WITH GUNS BLAZING
MACHETE SYSTEM
BOUNTY HUNTER – BOOK 3

BY ZEN DIPIETRO & M. D. COOPER

ZEN DIPIETRO & M. D. COOPER

Just in Time (JIT) & Beta Readers

Marti Panikkar
Steven Blevins
Manie Kilian
Scott Reid
Gene Bryan

Copyright © 2018 Zen DiPietro & M. D. Cooper
Aeon 14 is Copyright © 2018 M. D. Cooper
Version 1.0.0

ISBN: 978-1-64365-004-3

Cover Art by Andrew Dobell
Editing by Tee Ayer

Aeon 14 & M. D. Cooper are registered trademarks of Michael Cooper
All rights reserved

TABLE OF CONTENTS

PREVIOUSLY... 5
A DAY AT THE BEACH...7
SCHRAMM 21
OPTIONS 31
SAFE AS HOUSES..45
EYES EVERYWHERE 69
VISITORS 81
ARRANGEMENTS 91
INCOMMUNICADO 106
BACKEND OF NOWHERE..114
RECOVERY...143
PICKING FRUIT 158
BOLT HOLE 179
FURTHER ARRANGEMENTS 194
THE DEAL 215
THE BOOKS OF AEON 14..235
ALSO BY ZEN DIPIETRO 241
ABOUT THE AUTHORS 243

PREVIOUSLY...

Reece lives in a system named Machete, deep in the Perseus Expansion Districts. The PED is a region of the Orion Freedom Alliance that can best be described as the East Germany of the galaxy.

Here technology is limited, and people live a simpler life than is found in the Inner Stars or the Transcend—which is exactly how Praetor Kirkland of the Orion Freedom Alliance likes it.

In Reece's previous adventures she was sent on a hunt for a missing researcher along with a new—and largely unwanted—partner, Trey. Utilizing her network of contacts, Reece followed her prey out of the Machete System, and eventually returned him to her world of Akonwara.

Through the course of the mission, she grew to like Trey, and now the pair of them work together for Rexcare, one of the Big Four corporations that run the Machete System.

Following that mission, Reece and Trey had to get to the bottom of an attack on Reece's favorite whiskey distillery, Hatchet and Pipe.

They put that mystery to rest and saved the distillery from any harm. While doing so, their corporate sponsor, Schramm Mathews, had begun to behave strangely. Not so much that Reece was too concerned, but enough that she suspected that something may come up before long....

A DAY AT THE BEACH

DATE: 05.23.8948 (Adjusted Gregorian)
LOCATION: Tommy's Gun Shop, Ohiyo, Akonwara
REGION: Machete System, PED 4B, Orion Freedom Alliance

"When I said we should enjoy a nice vacation, this isn't what I had in mind." Trey's voice conveyed a puzzled mix of amusement and disappointment.

Reece paused to look up at him, a plasma-lance rocket-pod launcher balanced on her shoulder. Truth be told, she felt quite formidable at the moment, and she doubted any fun-in-the-starslight spot could match the feeling of more power and *bwa-ha-ha*-ness of holding the weapon

"You got upgraded to weapon-carrying status," she reminded him. "What could be better than following up on that?"

Trey shrugged. "Sand between my toes, the gentle roar of waves, and a cold beer while I refuse to look at the chronometer all day long?"

Actually, that did sound nice, but they were here for a purpose. Reece reluctantly handed the plasma lance launcher back to her old acquaintance, Tommy. Today wasn't the day to dream, apparently.

Instead, she moved to the other side of the smallish but well-equipped storeroom—where the pistols lay—while Tommy watched from a distance, already familiar with her buying habit. "I guess it doesn't mean as much to you, not growing up the Machete System but being permitted to carry a weapon is a very big deal here. Just *having* one designates you as someone of importance. It's gotten me what I wanted lots of times."

Trey joined her, looking down at the hand guns on display. "I don't know. I just don't love weapons the way you do, I guess. Maybe it's because they're so common where I'm from."

She gave him a long, appraising look. "Maybe. Or it could be that you *are* a weapon. With your superior strength and reflexes and heat-seeking abilities and all that."

"I don't have heat-seeking abilities. I'm not a missile. I just have the ability to see thermal signatures, and..." he trailed off. "Yeah, I guess that counts as heat-seeking...."

Reece patted him on the shoulder. "You're becoming self-aware. That bodes well for you, but bad for humanity."

He laughed.

His humor was coming along.

Actually...Reece cracked a lot more jokes these days. Maybe it was *her* humor that was progressing—as a result of Trey's influence. Not that she'd ever admit that to him. He'd just get all smug about it.

Reece skimmed her hand over the display case as she looked at the contents within. Her eye caught on pure beauty and she stilled.

A pair of Rikulf Specials—quite similar to hers—lay there, resting serenely with the sort of aura only something truly magnificent emits.

Trey must have noticed her sudden lack of movement as he shifted closer and said, "Oh. Those are just like yours."

"Not *just like*," she corrected.

Reece felt a little peeved about his lack of knowledge regarding the finer details of weaponry, but she'd let that pass. For now. Instead, this could be a teachable moment.

"Mine are optimized for heat dissipation and accuracy. That makes them a good choice for sudden use and sustained use, both of which are highly likely scenarios for me. These two here," she tapped the case with her forefinger, "have been retrofitted for larger, higher velocity rounds. It takes a deadeye to use them, but they sure pack a punch."

Trey pursed his lips, his brow creasing as he stared intently at the pistols on display. "You can tell all that just by looking at them? I mean, they really do look *just like yours.*"

Reece let out a small breath, trying not to feel too disappointed in him. What was the sense in Trey having those mods built into his body if he couldn't even appreciate the finer points of personal protection? "Yes. Here, I'll show you."

She glanced at Tommy, who quickly opened the case, tossed a shiny black cloth over it, then gently lay the pistols on top.

Reece drew her right-hand pistol—which she privately thought of as Righty—from its holster and aligned it with the model on the counter. "See this tiny ridge?"

She pointed at the barrel of her gun, then to the other weapon. "This one doesn't have it. That tells me it's been retrofitted with a barrel that has a greater internal width, allowing for a larger bullet." She tapped the back end of the weapon for sale, just above the hand grip. "And here. If we turn them and look down the two guns' profiles, you'll see that this one is slightly wider than mine. That gives it the bigger boom to launch that bigger bullet."

Trey nodded. "Ahh, now you're using technical terms like 'boom'. I see."

"I thought it would be best if I used words you'd understand," she teased. "Anyway, this set would be perfect for you."

"But it's like your set," he said, showing a disheartening lack of passion for these fine works of art. "I think I should have something different."

"These are different," she argued. "Your visual acuity makes you ideally suited for this pair. I wouldn't be nearly as good with these as you would be."

Secretly, she felt like she probably could match him at the shooting range, even with the other guns. An appeal to his ego couldn't hurt, though.

"Still," he said slowly. "Seems odd for us to be all matchy-matchy."

Tommy had stood by quietly up until this point, but he hurried to say, "These are a rare find. Since so few people are licensed to carry projectile weapons, it's a low-volume business that tends to require special ordering anything like Rikulfs. I only have these because they were part of a refurbishing lot I purchased from a merchant who was passing through Machete."

Trey shrugged. "I don't put a lot of stock in what's rare, or what's trendy, or any of that."

Frustratingly, Trey continued moving down the case,

gazing at the various items on display.

Tommy blinked in confusion, then quickly put a hand on Trey's arm to keep him from moving away.

Trey stopped and looked at the hand.

Tommy snatched back his hand, now a little flustered as he said, "I'll cut you a great deal on the Rikulfs. You'll get a huge value. Otherwise, I'll be sitting on them for months waiting for another buyer with an executive-carry license to come along and want something this powerful."

Trey hesitated. He looked at Reece, then Tommy. "I do have limited finances, since I so recently moved here. I barely even have any furniture in my new house."

Instead of renting the house in Reece's neighborhood, Trey had purchased it outright, saying he preferred to own what he used. The result of which was a sad lack of furnishings for his new home.

Trey shrugged at Reece. "I guess if you can make sure it's the best possible deal, I'll take them, even though I don't especially like them. I have to think about my finances ahead of my desires."

He had to have his arm twisted in order to agree to own two of the finest pistols this side of the Machete System? The man was impossible.

But the bargaining table had been set. Tommy named a price that Reece laughed at, and she named an insultingly low sum in response.

Back and forth, parry and lunge, and in less than two minutes, Reece had secured the weapons for Trey at a tremendous value.

As he paid for them, she said, "Once your finances are

in better shape, if you want to get something else, I'll buy these from you."

Trey shrugged. "I'm sure they'll be fine. It's not like I think I'll need to use them."

Reece stared at him. "There are times when I think we're getting along great, and then you go and say something like that."

He grinned.

Trey seemed to have more fun selecting the color and style of the weapon holster she'd negotiated into the price. In the end, he chose a waist-worn type, similar to the one Reece wore.

"Thanks, Tommy," she said. "At least he's wearing something respectable, even if he doesn't truly appreciate the Rikulfs."

She shook Tommy's hand and she exited the shop with Trey, who now wore his corporate-sanctioned firepower.

As they walked outside, she had to wonder if it was the harsh light of the perihelion alignment that made him suddenly much better looking.

Odd. For a second, she could almost see what Raya saw in him.

Trey smiled as they walked to the metro station.

"What?" she demanded.

"We were like peanut butter and crackers back there, like we've been partners for a decade. You really went along with my whole disinterested buyer thing. Tommy totally bought it."

"Oh. Right." She pretended she'd known all along what he'd been up to.

"It gives me a good feeling about our future endeavors together."

"Sure," Reece agreed.

"But I still think we need a team-building exercise. Something to really cement our partner bond, you know?"

She sighed, knowing exactly what he was driving at. "You want to go to the beach."

He pointed at her. "Bingo."

She sighed again. "And you're going to insist that I come, aren't you?"

"Oh, yeah. Definitely."

"Sand is bad for guns," she pointed out.

"So, we'll leave them locked up inside," he answered reasonably.

"We should invite Raya." With a stroke of genius, she realized that if Raya kept Trey busy, he'd have less time to insist Reece have fun out in the blistering heat.

"Great!" he enthused. "Now we're talking. We'll invite Kippy, too."

She cringed inwardly. Not that she didn't like the idea of spending time with Kippy, but they were on uncertain ground these days. Were they friends who had shared one hell of a kiss and a lot of increasing electricity, or had they passed over into some other relationship status?

Reece wasn't sure, and she didn't like things she wasn't sure about.

She tried to imagine what a trip to the beach with Trey, Kippy, Raya, and Dex would look like.

It would either be fantastic, or truly awful, but she could tell from the look on Trey's face that it was going to happen, one way or the other.

* * * * *

Reece had to admit that, when it came to sitting and doing nothing at all, Trey had it all figured out. Even she—who didn't care much for 'basking', has he called it—had begun to enjoy the fresh air, lovely view, and the sound of the waves rolling against the sandy beach.

After Trey had put up overhead heat-filtering screens and fans, that is. He'd brought chairs, too. Surprisingly comfortable folding lounge chairs.

"For a guy who claimed poverty at the security shop, you sure spent a lot on all this beach rig," she observed, sipping a pineapple and coconut drink he'd called a colada-something-or-other.

It was damned tasty.

"I invested in my future, because my future involves a lot of days on the beach," he said.

Raya tilted her head so that the wide brim of her hat cleared her vision enough that she could see Reece. "He makes a good point. It's been ages since I took a lazy day off. I need to do this more often."

She let out a blissful sigh and sank back into her chaise.

Raya's hat was the most substantial piece of apparel she wore. As soon as her sandaled feet had hit the sand, the woman had stripped off her coverup and revealed a bright red bikini that had made even Reece stumble when she saw it.

Kippy lounged next to Reece, looking as happy as

she'd ever seen him. She didn't think it was because of the bikini, though. Somehow, Kippy always seemed to be looking somewhere other than in Raya's general direction. During conversation, Reece noted that his gaze went directly to her face, then swung away.

She had the feeling he was doing it for her benefit, even though he made it seem completely natural.

Reece smiled and sipped her colada-whatever.

Dex chirped at her and she looked down to see him, bright-eyed, bushy-tailed, and holding out a perfect sea shell to her.

"Thanks, Dex. Good boy." She took the shell and he chittered happily, then scampered a few meters away.

Who ever heard of a monkey that liked hunting seashells?

"We should have invited Schramm," Trey said, drawing her attention from the monkey she'd grown quite fond of.

Reece chuckled. "Schramm Matthews at the beach? I can't imagine it. I'm pretty sure he's had his business suit permanently embedded into his skin, for ease of use."

"Have you ever seen him outside of work?" Trey asked.

"Sure. We've had lunch or dinner on numerous occasions. But it was only because he has to eat and meeting while he gathered sustenance was the most effective use of his time."

"I'm glad I'm not an exec," Raya said. "I don't mind working round the clock for short periods of time, but to have that be my way of life? I can't imagine it. It's no wonder so few execs get married, and if they do, they tend to marry other execs within the same company."

Reece snagged on the topic of marriage before anyone could move the conversation onward. "Do you have plans to get married, then?"

Raya laughed. "Someday, maybe. I don't know. But I like that it's a possibility, whether I ever do or not. That's the fun part of life—seeing what happens. I can't imagine leading a completely inflexible life, like an exec."

"I'll agree with that." Kippy stared out at the waves ahead. Every now and then, a big one brought a thin river of water up to the ends of their chairs, before the wave quickly receded and the sand began to visibly dry under the heat of the two stars glaring down from above. "Possibility is what makes life worth living."

"Count me in. I'll agree, too." Trey stood. "I'm going to go take a splash. The canopy and fans make the heat bearable, but a good soaking is all the better. Who's with me?"

Raya flipped up the top of her hat to gaze up at him. "I would, but I'd have to take my sandals off, and then the sand would burn my feet."

Trey pretended to give that some serious consideration, with one hand on his chin. "I could carry you to the water."

"Sure, that'll work." Raya gazed up at him coyly, kicking off her sandals.

Trey bent and scooped her up. "Off we go, then. Pineapple!"

He trotted the few steps into the surf, then waded out

waist-deep, still carrying Raya, who was laughing and kicking her bare feet.

"Pineapple?" Kippy asked, an eyebrow raised.

"It's his idea of a rabble-rouser. Something to say when things are going to get exciting."

"Ah. He's funny."

"I know, but don't tell him that. It would only encourage him." Reece smiled.

Kippy watched the pair out ahead, now splashing each other with water and laughing. "They seem really well suited."

"They do, oddly enough. Who would have thought?"

"Does it bother you?' he asked.

"What for them to date? No. Why would it?"

Kippy only shrugged in response.

Dex came loping back with something clutched to his chest, but what he handed her wasn't a shell. It was a thumbnail-sized piece of green glass, polished smooth by the water and sand.

"Good boy, Dex. Come and have some water. I don't know how fast you get dehydrated, but better to be safe." She emptied a water pouch into a cup and held it for him. After giving a curious look, he lowered his head and drank.

"How much do you think he understands?" Kippy straightened and turned sideways, letting his legs hang over the side of his lounger.

"I haven't figured it out yet. Sometimes he seems to pick a word out that I wouldn't have expected, and other times he pretends he doesn't know what I'm saying when I know he does."

Kippy chuckled. "Sounds like he's pretty smart, then. What's that he gave you?"

"Sea glass." She put it on her palm and held it out to him. "Surprisingly pretty, isn't it? Almost like a gem, even though it's just glass."

He plucked it from her hand and examined it. "Yeah, it is pretty."

She sat on the edge of her chair, sideways like him, expecting him to keep talking. But he went quiet, and she couldn't think of anything to add.

Reece looked down at Dex to avoid making eye contact with Kippy. Somehow, looking him in the eye and not talking felt like something…kind of dangerous—and not in a good way.

In a scary way. A what-if-I-screw-this-up-and-we-can't-ever-go-back way.

She couldn't imagine her life without the funny, warm, loyal, man sitting across from her. And when had he gotten so sexy? That was kind of a problem for her at the moment, since he'd gone shirtless and shoeless, and looked entirely like he needed her hands on his tanned skin.

But if she did that, and they became a couple, and things went wrong, she'd lose the person she cared about most.

"I think I'll go cool off, too." Before he could answer, she hurriedly shrugged off her lightweight coverup. Her sea green bikini was a much more sporty type than Raya's red scraps. It was the kind of thing she could play beach volleyball in or do some tai chi or something.

All the better for her way of life. She'd never be

comfortable wearing something that could have the slightest shift and give her a massive wedgie.

The idea of Raya with a monster wedgie made her laugh as she splashed out into the water.

Kippy came running behind her, then dove under an incoming wave that she let carry her backward two steps.

"What's so funny?" he asked catching sight of her grin.

"Butts."

"Butts?" He looked bewildered, but amused. "Like…your butt?"

"No! My butt has never done anything funny, ever."

His mouth twisted. "Well, there was that one time at school in our sixth year,"

She'd waded out chest deep by that point, and let her knees buckle to plunge her beneath the water, letting the waves wash over her and end the annoying conversation.

* * * * *

Trey had planned their day at the beach so well that he'd even rented a storage space near the shore to hold the chairs, fans, and other supplies.

It saved them from the worst part of going to the beach: hauling sandy stuff back to your home.

Tired from all the relaxation and fun, Reece immediately felt lulled by the motion of the autotaxi. She let Kippy, Raya, and Trey's conversation become white noise and drifted off.

When awareness returned, Reece realized she'd leaned over in her sleep, and her head now rested on Kippy's shoulder.

He smelled nice.

He also hadn't moved her.

She kept her eyes closed and stayed that way for an extra minute before drawing in a deep breath and sitting up. They were about to arrive at the metro station. She didn't have any message alerts, but she checked her queues anyway via her Link.

Nothing. Kind of strange. She'd put in a call to Schramm two days ago to see if he'd be okay with her taking a proper vacation for a few days—maybe even going to visit Ed.

Schramm had warned her that he'd be extremely busy for the next couple of weeks, but he'd never gone so long without returning a call.

She shoved her feet into her shoes and reached for her bag as the autotaxi pulled up to the station.

She'd enjoyed taking some time to relax today and suspected it would be good for her if she did more of that kind of thing. But as she left the autotaxi, her mind was already filled with concern at Schramm's strange absence.

If she didn't hear from her boss the next day, she'd go see him in person.

SCHRAMM

DATE: 05.24.8948 (Adjusted Gregorian)
LOCATION: Rexcare HQ, Ohiyo, Akonwara
REGION: Machete System, PED 4B, Orion Freedom Alliance

"What do you mean, 'he's not in'? He's always in." A wave of suspicion rolled through Reece.

Tavin rolled his shoulders in a tiny shrug. "You're having some time off. Why shouldn't he?"

In the lobby of Rexcare, Reece faced off against the dragons' lair of receptionists who controlled access to the entire building and all the people within. Reece and Tavin had always had a good relationship, but he seemed a little too nonchalant about Schramm's absence.

At the very least, Tavin should know when Schramm would return. Yet he didn't offer that information, which meant he didn't know it—or wasn't sharing.

Reece's suspicion morphed into unease. Something wasn't right.

"I'd like to see Erving, then," Reece decided. Schramm's personal assistant would know anything there was to know.

"I'll see if he's free." Tavin gave her a small, apologetic smile.

A moment later, Tavin nodded and gestured to the elevator bank. "Go on up. Car four."

At least one thing was going right. Reece let out a breath as she waited for elevator four's doors to open. The fact that she didn't have unfettered access to the building usually didn't rub her the wrong way, but today it did.

Shouldn't I be able to come and go as I please? she thought as the doors opened and she stepped into the elevator.

Of course not. She wasn't an exec, or the support staff of an exec. Such a vaunted status would never be hers.

She snorted.

When the doors opened on her destination level, she strode directly to Erving's office. He looked up and smiled when she entered, and she instantly knew something was off. She couldn't put her finger on what, or why she felt that way—maybe it was because Erving so rarely smiled.

Rather than waste time with pleasantries, Reece got right to the point. "What the hell's going on? Where's Schramm?"

Erving blinked, but recovered quickly. "Mr. Matthews is working out of the office."

"On what?" Reece demanded.

"I can't disclose that."

Reece took a step closer, not blinking and not breaking eye contact. "You'd better."

Erving's Adam's apple bobbed up and down as the man swallowed hard.

Oh, good. He responded to directness and a threatening manner. That was fortunate, because those two traits were right in her wheelhouse.

Reece pushed her right hip forward and half-sat on the front of Erving's desk, causing him to push his chair back a half meter while he stared up at her.

"You and I have been working for Schramm, together

but entirely separate, for how long now?" she asked. "Three years? Four? You must know by now that when shit goes wrong, I'm the one Schramm calls to clean it up."

She paused. Actually, that wasn't the mental image she'd intended to create, but the damage was done now.

"What I mean is, there's nothing on the gray side of things I haven't seen. No secret I haven't squashed. No lie I haven't told. If Schramm is in a tight spot, I need to know, so I can go in with guns blazing and get him out."

To underscore her words, she flipped her jacket open to better show Lefty, snugly holstered in her weapons belt.

Like most citizens who didn't see genuine firepower on a daily basis, Erving focused on the pistol.

"Figuratively speaking, of course," she added. "Unless the situation calls for actual weaponry. But I won't know that until you tell me. Either way, think about it. Is there anyone more qualified to help Schramm with whatever's gone wrong than me?"

Erving's eyes popped up from Lefty to meet Reece's gaze, then returned to Lefty, and then flicked to the left in the unmistakable gesture of someone checking their Link.

Reece waited.

Erving hesitated.

Hesitation was good. It meant a wavering of one's resolve. But it was important not to push too hard, too fast, and risk pushing someone to become defensive.

"Schramm's important to me, too, you know," she said confidentially. "On a personal level. He's the one who brought me in here, and the one who has stood by my—sometimes unconventional—methods. You know I'm loyal to him, beyond anything else."

Beyond the company, in other words. Beyond Rexcare.

It was a dangerously bold statement, and it caught Erving's attention. He stared at her, blinking rapidly, as if he were a computer processing a great deal of data all at once.

Trust me, she silently implored.

Erving folded his hands in his lap. "Well… the truth is, I don't know where he is."

It was Erving's job to know every excruciating detail about Schramm's life, both professional and not. Alarm bells, sirens, and claxons went off in Reece's mind, but she remained still, with an outward appearance of calm. "Has that ever happened before?"

"No." Erving's eyes widened a hair, revealing his fear.

"Why haven't you called in help to look for him? What if he's been injured or something?" Reece's own concern rose like a mushroom cloud in her brain.

Erving's eyes darted to the left, then to the right, and then they widened into big circles.

After a moment of confusion, Reece understood. He had something to say, but feared saying it within Rexcare, where someone might be listening.

A realization made her chest feel heavy. This was bigger than she'd thought. She pointed to the door and Erving nodded.

Reece went through the motions of thanking Erving

for his help while he offered to share her elevator on his way downstairs. They got into the elevator and descended in silence.

Once out on the street, they still said nothing. Erving pointed in the direction of the metro station and she understood. In a strange, silent agreement, they boarded the first available metro train, took it to its first stop, and disembarked. Once on the street again, they ducked down a service alley where—finally— Erving seemed willing to speak aloud.

Sort of. His voice barely reached a whisper. His fear and paranoia were evident, and—considering what he must know about the inner workings of Rexcare—that scared the hell out of Reece.

"Things aren't right," he whispered.

"What things?" she hissed back. She wasn't good at whispering. Her volume sounded more like a stage whisper.

"I have to get back in the office before they realize I've gone out for more than just a drink or to grab some lunch," he said. "Meet me tonight, somewhere off the Rexcare grid."

"The Debtor's Haven," she said immediately. She could think of nowhere more acutely aware of the need of privacy and a lack of monitoring devices. "At 20:00."

Erving nodded. "Don't go anywhere unusual. Don't say anything to anyone that they might hear. They'll be listening. Be careful."

Reece frowned. "I will. You be careful, too."

He nodded. "I'll take the train back. You wait and take a train to some other destination before heading to wherever you really want to go. Understand?"

"Yeah. I understand."

Erving nodded again, looking grim but satisfied. He strode away without looking back.

Well, hell. What is going on?

* * * * *

"You seem tense, honey." Aunt Ruth looked at Reece, a concerned frown wrinkling her brow. "You barely touched your seafood burrito, and you love those."

Aunt Ruth wasn't the only one who had picked up on Reece's unease. Rio had curled up in her lap—something he normally only did when she was sick.

"It's just work," Reece said lightly, scratching Rio's ears. "You know how it is with some jobs."

Aunt Ruth nodded, but didn't look entirely convinced. "Well, I'll wash up the dishes. Should have them done in time for *The Zillion Prize*. Why don't you watch with me?"

Aunt Ruth wanted to keep an eye on her. It was sweet. Reece picked Rio up. "Sure. I'll go put it on. But I can do the dishes, too."

"Nope. You'll just put them in the autowash. I like washing the dishes. It reminds me of when I was a young girl."

Reece felt bad about leaving the tedious job to Aunt Ruth. Still, if her aunt truly wanted to do it, Reece shouldn't deprive her of it. "Okay. I'll go get your show ready."

The blinking lights, silly exploits, and inane chatter of

the game show might take her mind off whatever was going on with Schramm.

At least, she hoped it would.

*****

Trey met Reece at the Debtor's Haven.

"No Dex?" Reece asked, since Trey tended to bring Dex to most places he went.

"I didn't like your tone when you told me about this meeting," he said. "I thought it best to leave Dex at home. Besides, I took him to the park and he climbed so many trees he's exhausted."

"My tone?" she asked. "We talked via the Link. In text."

He shrugged. "You still had tone."

How she could have a tone when communicating via text, she couldn't fathom, but since leaving Dex behind was probably the right choice, she decided to let it go.

They hadn't gotten three meters into the betting lounge when Marky greeted them, hugging first Reece, then Trey.

"No Dex?" she asked.

Reece wondered if Marky was making conversation, or actually disappointed—Reece would bet on the latter.

"Not tonight," Trey said. "How's the gaming?"

"Fantastic. Got a couple of high rollers playing some King Sweep. There's a big take building." Marky smiled. "Care to get in on it?"

"Not sure I'll be able to," Trey said. "We don't know how long our meeting will take."

Marky nodded. "The back room is ready for you. Take all the time you need. But if you get a chance, join my table. I'm confident you'd come out ahead."

"Doesn't it violate some sort of ethics to give advice like that?" Reece demanded. She didn't actually mind if the house stacked the deck—figuratively speaking, of course—in favor of its friends. It was fun to have a chance to tease Marky, though.

"Betting lounges and ethics aren't the closest of acquaintances," Marky drawled. She winked, then moved past them to greet someone else who'd just arrived.

It wasn't Erving.

Reece didn't know who the new arrival was, but judging by the amount of attention Marky gave her, the woman must be a regular at the Debtor's Haven.

"Where do you want to wait?" Trey asked.

"In the room. I don't think I'd have any fun playing games while we wait."

"That bad, huh?" He started back toward the room.

One nice thing about traveling with Trey was that, even in a crowded place, when people saw him coming, they immediately got out of his way.

Reece kind of envied that. People would move for her, too, but she had to project a whole lot of disgruntlement, and even then, sometimes she had to make sure her guns were visible.

The back room didn't offer much more than a table and chairs. After twenty minutes, Reece had gotten bored. After forty, she'd started to get annoyed. An hour after the proscribed meeting time, she had become worried.

She didn't want to contact Erving via the Link—just in case someone at Rexcare might be monitoring his communications. That would be highly illegal, of course, but also par for the course for a corporation.

"What should we do?" Trey asked.

"Go ahead and play some King Sweep. I'll stay here and wait."

"You sure?" He didn't move from his chair.

"Yeah. There's no sense in both of us sitting here and staring at the walls."

"You're such a star." He gave her head a pat as he got up and left.

After a second hour, she gave up hope that Erving would come. But she had to find out why he hadn't.

She caught Trey's eye as she crossed the lounge and he nodded. A minute later—after playing his hand—he closed out his winnings device by transferring everything to his personal account.

Since Marky was busy running the King Sweep game, Reece simply waved at her before leaving.

After a short walk, they arrived at the metro station. Going to Erving's apartment was risky—since cameras might record their presence—but it was a better option than electronic communication, in which every word had the potential of being recorded.

Reece hurried toward the Metro's scanners. Using her credentials, she always swept through them without even having to pause.

Except this time, the scanner beeped and refused to open. Trey bumped into her from behind as she came to a sudden stop.

The system had experienced a temporary glitch. Things like that happened sometimes.

But when she tried again, she got the same dismissive beep.

"What's wrong?" Trey asked.

"Try yours," she said, moving out of his way.

He got the same result.

She stilled her mind amid the whirlwind of horror and shock that went through her. "We have to go back out. They'll know we're at the station. They'll note what we're doing and where we're going."

Without hesitation, Trey reversed course and she hurried after him.

"Who is 'they'?" he asked as they hustled out.

"There are only a few possibilities," she said, thinking aloud. "It has to be someone at the top of Rexcare."

They got back out to the street and waved down an unoccupied taxi.

"Any idea what's going on?" Trey asked as it pulled up to the curb.

"No," she said tersely. "But whatever 'it' is, it involves Schramm and Erving, too."

They got into the taxi and went silent, not wanting to be overheard by the driver. At the moment, she didn't even feel comfortable using her Link. Though the hardware resided in her body, Rexcare had purchased it—which meant it could have any number of monitoring devices built in. She'd never minded that before, since there had never been anything she'd wanted to hide that Rexcare didn't also want to remain willfully ignorant of.

That might no longer be the case.

She decided that she had two top priorities. First, she and Trey had to get off the grid, where Rexcare couldn't find them.

The second priority would ensure that they could remain off the grid—which posed its own dangers.

They needed to jailbreak her Link.

OPTIONS

DATE: 05.24.8948 (Adjusted Gregorian)
LOCATION: Tommy's Gun Shop, Ohiyo, Akonwara
REGION: Machete System, PED 4B, Orion Freedom Alliance

"I didn't expect to see you back so soon." Tommy didn't seem at all surprised by the fact that people would show up at his shop at such a strange hour. No doubt that was standard operating procedure for him. He did seem puzzled and concerned when he realized who his visitors were, though.

He continued, "If there's something wrong with the Rikulfs, I'll take care of it for you. I can fix just about any weapon or security device."

Reece closed and locked the door behind them. "That's why we're here. But not because of the Rikulfs. I need you to jailbreak my Link."

Tommy sucked in a breath. "Of all the things I expected you to say, that wasn't one of them."

"I bet. But you did say there was nothing you couldn't do with a security device."

Tommy pulled at his earlobe. "That wasn't exactly what I said. And a proprietary Link inside someone's head isn't the same thing as an anti-theft system."

Reece didn't have time to argue with him. "I'll put it this way. I'm convinced that my safest course of action right now is to let you jailbreak a device that's directly connected to my nervous system. Do you think it's a good idea for me to remain here longer than necessary, with the Link active as it is right now, while we debate the finer points of safety?"

Tommy tightened his jaw. "Good point. This way."

Without waiting to see if they followed, he crossed the shop and opened the door to the back.

The door he never let anyone else go through.

In spite of the situation, Reece felt the thrill of finally being able to see what was behind the door.

As she found herself looking at a short hallway with a bathroom at one end and an apparent storage room at the other, Reece felt mildly disappointed.

She and Trey followed Tommy into the storage room, where they went straight to the back wall and proceeded halfway down the row of shelves, then stopped.

Tommy reached out and grabbed the edge of a two-meter section of shelving. Like all the others in the room, it held a variety of bins and boxes.

The section shelving of slid out from the wall without too much difficulty. Reece stepped back in surprise. There had been nothing that indicated the section wasn't solidly attached to the shelves on either side.

She stepped around Tommy, intrigued that he'd revealed a door, but before she could ask any questions, he yanked it open and went in.

Reece glanced over her shoulder at Trey. If they had been using their Link, she was pretty sure he'd make some crack about not being too sure about disappearing into a back room with this dude.

He remained silent, though, looking intense but calm.

She liked that he kept hold of himself when shit got serious. It boded well for what was to come.

She stepped into the hidden room, which was larger

than she'd expected. Judging by the size, it ran the entire length of the building, though it was only a couple meters wide. The walls, floor, and ceiling were all covered in a shiny gray material.

Tommy closed the door. "I have a lot of dampening in here. EM signals can't get in or out. So we're safe to work. Though, if they tracked you here and are on their way right now, we're kind of screwed. Is that a possibility?"

Was it? Reece looked a Trey, who gazed back at her.

"I think it's unlikely," she decided. "They'd be more interested in tracking me, *then* acquiring me if they don't come up with anything useful. But I don't know anything for sure at the moment."

Trey held up a hand. "Do you think they revoked our metro passes to agitate us and see what we'd do?"

"That's my suspicion," Reece said. "That they hope we'll lead them somewhere."

Trey stared at her blankly, then his eyes widened. "To Schramm. Right?"

She hadn't had time to think it through that far, but when she added up Schramm's absence, Erving's nervousness and failure to show up at their meeting, and then the voiding of their metro passes, it all seemed to fall into place. "It seems likely."

Tommy had gone to the far end of the room, where a long table took up the entire length of the short wall. "So, we're doing this?" he asked over his shoulder.

"Yeah. What do we need to do?"

"Help me clear this table." He began taking bins off it and setting them a couple meters away.

When the table was clear, Tommy opened one of the bins he'd moved and handed Reece a spray bottle. "Spray the table down to sanitize it."

She looked at the bottle and wondered if the sanitizing agent Rexcare was working to develop from barley enzymes would have been superior—if it were available. With a glance at Trey, she could tell he was wondering the same thing.

Funny. Compared to what they now faced, their job figuring out what had happened to Hatchet and Pipe seemed like good times.

Reece sanitized the table, as directed. Meanwhile, Tommy rummaged through bins, pulling things out and setting them aside.

"Now lie down," he said.

Trey approached. "Just how dangerous is this?"

Tommy began setting machinery on the table. The odd assortment of relatively square and rectangular things, with a few long, pointy things appeared somewhat alarming.

Reece stopped looking at them. It wouldn't help. Instead, she turned her face to the ceiling and closed her eyes. "Depends on whether they included anti-tamper hardware. If they did—and we trigger it—it could cause serious damage to my nervous system. I don't think Rexcare would do that to me, though."

"Because they so clearly have great loyalty to you?" Trey asked, sarcastically.

"No. Because it costs a lot, and I'm not really worth the effort." Reece doubted that her assessment made Trey feel better, but she derived a little comfort from it.

On the other hand, she felt pretty sure that Rexcare had probably included some covert monitoring capabilities in her Link implants. Since she was a fixer, and privy to intimate details about the company that others—outside of the highest-level execs—were not, it made practical sense to install such a failsafe. Knowing that wasn't the least bit comforting.

All the more reason to get this done quickly.

"So what does the best-case scenario look like, here?" Trey asked.

"You have a Link, right?" Tommy asked Trey. "Probably way more sophisticated than hers, even."

Reece opened her eyes to look at Trey. He never talked to people about his augments. Not only because of his personal history and feelings about augments, but also because people in Machete looked at such things far differently than his people did.

Trey tensed and looked down at the floor. "Yes. More sophisticated, but not proprietary. None of this corporate booby-trapping."

Tommy turned his full attention on Trey. "Actually..." He trailed off, looking intently at Trey, apparently thinking something through. "Actually, we can use that. I assume you're able to establish a point-to-point connection that doesn't use Akon's network?"

"Sure."

"That's great. We can connect you to Reece and you can be in contact with her while we do this. Normally we'd do it via the usual means but using any part of the local network would be a bad idea, for obvious reasons. Since Reece will be paralyzed while I work on her, she won't be able to speak to us."

"Paralyzed?" Trey asked.

Tommy nodded. "Yeah. I don't know how your people do it, but here, we need all voluntary and involuntary movement stopped to be able to work on the neural connections. The only movement she'll have will be for breathing."

Trey studied Reece, as if trying to gauge how disturbing that reality was for her.

She didn't love it, but there was nothing she could do about it. She gave Trey a tiny nod to assure him that she was okay.

"All right. Let's do what we need to do and get this over with." Trey had moved on to her own way of looking at the situation.

Tommy lifted an injector and moved to stand next to Reece. "First, I'm going to give you a relaxant. Then we'll do the paralytic. It's a bad feeling to lose control of your body, and a lot of people flip out over it.

"Fine. Let's just get going." Reece closed her eyes again and felt a light, brief pressure on her neck.

Tommy said, "While that takes effect, Trey, establish a Link with her. Both of you need to keep it open. If you close it, you might not be able to reestablish it until the paralytic wears off."

<Hey.> Trey's voice came directly into her mind. He didn't often use the ability to do that, mostly because she didn't like it. But today, she didn't mind that he'd be inside her head with her while Tommy worked on her implants.

<Hey,> she answered back, via text. She wondered if

the text translated into some sort of voice, in his mind. She'd have to ask him about it later.

<You sure you want this guy tinkering around in your head?> Trey asked. <Not to alarm you, but the dude looks more like a tattoo artist than a brain surgeon, to me.>

Reece laughed. Oh. The relaxant must have started to work. She felt kind of...groovy. It was nice, really.

<He's a lot more capable than he looks. That's part of the point.>

<Oh, so that's his disguise?> Trey asked.

With her eyes closed, she smiled. If he was trying to distract her by being funny, he was doing a marvelous job. <I always thought he looked kind of cool, in an I-care-little-for-hygiene sort of way.>

<I feel like this is a theme for you,> Trey commented. <Making friends with people who have personal hygiene issues. Like that discredited doctor friend of yours. The one who didn't care for wearing pants.>

<Coocoo. He's a discredited nurse, but yeah, he feels pants are overrated. And things turned out well with that. Your cosmetic overlays work perfectly, when you choose to wear them.>

"You ready for the paralytic?" Tommy asked.

"Ready as I'm going to get," Reece said aloud.

She felt Tommy's hand on her neck. "Try to stay relaxed."

Reece tried. She tried her very best. But as soon as the pressure at her neck left, she felt a streak of panic, knowing that her body was about to become completely beyond her control. She waited for a tingle or something, but nothing happened. She felt normal.

She flexed her hands, but found them heavy, like they'd been encased in cement. Lifting her knees did nothing.

\<You okay?\> Trey asked. \<You got quiet.\>

His voice chased away the panic.

\<I'm okay. It's just weird. I know you're right beside me, but I feel like a huge barrier has appeared between me and everything out there.\>

\<There's no barrier. I'm right here. My hand is on your shoulder.\>

"Is she okay?" Tommy asked.

"She's fine," Trey answered. "It takes more than a little paralysis to keep her down."

Reece laughed to herself inside her mind.

"Good," Tommy said. "Move aside, please, and stay back. Don't accidentally touch me."

\<He thinks he's my type,\> Trey said to Reece, somehow managing to sound confidential even over the Link.

She again felt like laughing. \<Tell me something.\>

\<Okay. I don't like the underwear selection on Akon. Everything's natural fiber. I grew up with synthetic fibers, and they're lighter weight. In Akon underpants, I feel like I'm wearing diapers.\>

Reece imagined him wearing a diaper. It was good that she was under the effects of a paralytic, because otherwise she would have laughed herself right off the table and no doubt caused Tommy to gouge holes in her brain, or burn it, or whatever.

\<Not that,\> she said. \<Though that is hilarious—I might never get the mental image out of my head. I meant tell me about something. Something from your past, or a story your

people like to tell. I just want you to talk for a long time, so I can think just about what you're saying.>

<Oh, I gotcha. Sure. I can do that.>

But their Link went silent.

<Hello?> she prompted. <*Getting my innards flushed out here, could use some entertainment.*>

<*Sorry. I'm just kind of stumped as what to tell you. I'm not much of a storyteller.*>

<*Then tell me something about your life. You almost never talk about your past. Tell me about something that happened to you once.*>

<Can I lie?> he asked.

<Sure.>

Tommy intruded on their conversation. "I'm going to install a second core for the implants, and then I'll be able to take control of Rexcare's proprietary bits."

<*Can you make him shut up?*> Reece asked. <*Hearing the status updates isn't going to help me.*>

"She'd prefer silence," Trey said.

"Oh. Okay. I'll be quiet unless I need her to do something."

<*What could I possibly do?*> she asked. <*Think really hard about my favorite flavor of container ice?*>

Reece heard Trey chuckle softly.

<*Maybe. But you wanted me to tell you about something, so here it is. When I was twelve, all the kids in my grade had a field trip to see a play in person. I don't even remember what the play was, or if I liked it, but afterward we had lunch at a restaurant. I ordered a strawberry milkshake, and it was huge. Too much to drink, so I took it with me to finish on the way back to school. By the time we got back, the other grades had*

been dismissed. After a flurry of arriving and leaving, the school got oddly quiet. A friend and I kind of stayed behind for no good reason except that we weren't in any hurry. We roamed the halls, pretending it was a post-apocalyptic warzone and weirding ourselves out.

<Anyway, I still carried that milkshake, and it had completely melted and wasn't cold anymore. And there we were, on the third floor, and a window was open. I don't know why, but it was just open. No screen or anything. Maybe it was being worked on or something. But I had that milkshake in one hand and that window right in front of me, and I thought, I wonder what it would be like to drop this three floors.

<So I did, and I have to admit, it was kind of glorious. The fall took longer than I thought it would, and the milkshake kind of poured out as it fell, making this long ribbons of pink in the air. Then it landed, and the whole thing just kind of exploded upward and outward. I learned a lesson about physics that day, and how much bigger half a cup of milkshake can look when it has been applied to a surface with force.

<We stood there looking out the window, impressed and horrified and suddenly terrified we'd get in trouble. So we casually—but quickly—went downstairs and out a different exit. But then we circled around the school to see the fallout at ground level, and let me tell you, it was even more spectacular. It was like someone had splattered the area with three gallons of pink paint, but the paint was sticky, and bound to attract ants at some point. It was all over the ground, up the steps, on the handrail, on the bike rack, out into the parking lot... There were pink speckles thirty feet away.

<The next morning at school, all the kids were talking about it. And my friend and I played dumb, pretending to be

as mystified as everyone else. Neither of us ever told anyone, as far as I know, until right now.>

Reece tried to imagine Trey as an adolescent, and had a hard time picturing it.

<You okay?>

<I'm still here, and still fine. I was just trying to picture you as a kid.>

<Big ears, hands too big for my arms, and kind of clumsy. It wasn't a beautiful sight. Best you put it out of your mind.>

<Okay. It's a fun story,> Reece said, wondering if she'd have agreeable 'tone'. <A good prank that caused some mayhem but no real damage.>

<Yeah. I really didn't expect it to be as big a thing as it turned out to be.>

<Is there a point to this story? Some sort of moral or thing you want to make me aware of?>

Trey gave an audible snort. <Are you kidding? You think I'm the old sage type who tells a story that makes everyone understand life a little bit better? You wanted a story. I thought that one would amuse you.>

<Ah. I see. Well, it did.>

<Although…if I were going to try to wring some sort of wisdom out of that story,> he continued, <I guess it would be that even a big mess can, ultimately, end up being harmless.>

<Are you talking about my brain? I feel like you're talking about my brain. And it's not cool to tell me my brain is a mess.>

<Uh…no,> Trey sounded awkward and nervous now. <I was thinking it might apply to this entire situation, but no, forget it. This story has no wisdom. Entirely wisdom-free nostalgia, nothing more.>

Reece wanted to sigh, but her body was busy pretending she didn't exist. <I see. Well, thanks, anyway. It was mildly diverting. What else do you have?>

<Uhh...how about the time I tried learning how to fish? Like, with string and stuff.>

<Sounds dreadful. Pass.>

Trey gave a rueful laugh. <Yeah, it was, actually. The live bait thing kind of freaked me out. How about the story of my first date?>

Reece most certainly did. <Now that sounds funny. Let's hear it.>

<No way. It did not go well. I was kidding about telling you that one.>

<Well that's bogus. And here I am, all helpless and sad, and you're teasing me with stories you won't actually tell.>

She heard him sigh.

<Put it this way. It ended with me accidentally putting my hand on her sister's ass, both of them thinking it was intentional, and me being labeled a perv.>

<How do you accidentally put your hand on someone's ass?> Reece wished she could speak audibly so she could apply the correct sardonic tone to the words.

<It's easier than you think when it's dark and someone has inexplicably stopped to adjust her shoe strap. But I'd rather not relive it, thank you very much.>

<And you were labeled a perv for accidentally bumping into someone in the dark?>

<Oh, yeah. They called me Trey, the bandit assgrabber. They even listed me that way in our senior yearbook. And thanks so much for making me relive it.>

<Well, **you** brought it up, not me.>

Trey grunted. <*That's just how dedicated a partner I am. You remember that.*>

<*Fine. I will.*>

<*Good.*>

<*My partner is a bandit assgrabber. It's hard to forget that. And good that I know, too. All this time I've been doing risky things like walking in front of you and leaving my backside entirely unattended.*>

<*Well, that's not fair,*> he protested. <*How can a backside be unattended? It's attached. You're right there.*>

<*But looking the other way entirely. And that's just how you like it, right?*>

She could hear him laughing, and wondered what Tommy thought about it.

"Okay," Tommy said. "That's it."

"That's it?" Trey repeated.

"Yep. I don't know what you two were talking about, but she was so relaxed, it went easy. No hangups or problems. Your Link is officially free of any Rexcare tampering."

Reece wanted to let out a breath of relief, but her face was still frozen.

"I'll give you the antidote to the paralytic. It'll take a while to wear off completely, though, and you need to wait until it's all gone before you try to get up."

"I'll make sure she waits," Trey said.

<*Or what? You'll grab my ass?*> She peeked through her eyelids for his reaction. Oh. That worked. She could move her eyelids.

He looked down at her with a stern glare, but she knew it was a fake.

She flapped her eyelids at him, since it was the only movement she could make.

<Actually,> she told him, <now that the iffy bit is over, all this stillness is kind of relaxing. I think I might take a nap.>

<You? Take a nap? What a surprise. What is it with you and naps, anyway?> Trey asked.

<Have you ever heard of an animal called a camel? They can drink crazy amounts of water and save it up so they don't have to drink for months.>

<Did Tommy tweak your brain? I don't see where you're going with this.>

<I'm like a camel with sleep. I store it up, and then can go without whenever I need.>

Trey groaned. <That's dumb, and not at all how humans work.>

<No, you're dumb. And a bandit assgrabber. Now shut up and let me sleep.>

Her lips twitched.

Apparently facial movement was coming back, too.

SAFE AS HOUSES

DATE: 05.24.8948 (Adjusted Gregorian)
LOCATION: Tommy's Gun Shop, Ohiyo, Akonwara
REGION: Machete System, PED 4B, Orion Freedom Alliance

"Ugh!" Reece put a hand to her back. "Ow! Why did you two let me sleep on a metal table? I feel like I've been worked over by a pair of drummers using me for the bass drum. Ow! Dammit!"

Tommy looked apologetic. "That's the aftereffect of the paralytic. You're going to be stiff and in pain for the next day or so. Nothing to do for it. Sorry."

She decided not to give him a stern talking-to about failing to warn her about that bit, since he'd really helped her out of a jam.

Besides, all things considered, things could have ended up a whole lot worse.

"Do you two need a place to stay?" Tommy asked.

"Uh." She hadn't thought that far ahead.

"I guess we do," Trey said. "We can't exactly just go back home if Rexcare's looking for us."

"Right." Reece considered their options.

"I have a safehouse you can use," Tommy offered. "Off the grid, no mainline connections, no cameras. It's out in an agricultural zone, but just barely, and I keep it stocked with food and everything you'll need. Even some good painkillers."

Reece didn't want to admit it, but as she stood hunched over, one hand on the edge of the table and trying not to move, she could really use some good painkillers.

"You don't mind getting mixed up in all this?" Trey asked.

Tommy shrugged. "I've been mixed up in just about everything at one point or another. The trick is not getting caught—and I never have. Good track record, right?"

"Yeah. You've got me sold." Trey sent Reece a questioning look.

"Yeah. Me too. Thanks, Tommy."

"No worries," Tommy said. "You'll get me back later. You always do. Besides, I think I owed you one or two."

More like three, since Reece liked to keep Tommy well in her debt, considering his usefulness. It had been an excellent strategy, and she was glad to be able to cash in on it now. "Can you get a message to someone for me? Off the grid."

"Sure." Tommy bent, rummaged in a bin, and pulled out a device. "Enter it and tell me where it needs to go."

She wrote a message to Kippy, telling him they had to go underground for a little while, and asking him to look after Aunt Ruth and Dex.

She hoped he wouldn't worry. But she often disappeared like this, so he should just assume this is like any other time she suddenly got pulled into something for work.

Handing the device back to Tommy, she realized she had nothing with her but the outfit she wore and her weapons. "I guess we'll need to stop off for some toothbrushes and some clothes and stuff."

Tommy waved her suggestion away. "What kind of

cheapo safehouse do you think I have? Everything you'll need is there. The clothes might not be awesome, but they'll be fine. Go. Be safe. Let me know if you need anything from me. I'll check in each day."

"Thanks, Tommy." She let out a breath. Just that morning, she'd been employed by Rexcare as a bounty hunter, and her life had been going well. How quickly everything could change.

"No problem. This is kind of my thing. Just let me lock up and I'll drive you to the autotaxi. You shouldn't use your accounts to buy things, so I'll give you access to one of my burner accounts and you can pay me back later."

"Thanks, but I have my own backup accounts. We'll be fine."

Tommy nodded. "Planning ahead. I like it. Let's go."

* * * * *

Reece wanted to get right to finding Schramm. She really did, but the trouble was that her whole body hurt so damn much she was operating at peak efficiency just to get herself into the nondescript little house on a nondescript little road that looked like all the other little houses and roads they'd passed for twenty minutes.

Which was a pretty good area setup for a safehouse.

She groaned as she sat down in a padded chair in the front room, holding her arms to her chest.

"I'll go find the painkillers." Trey looked concerned.

Reece didn't say anything. She simply sat, upright except for hunching over slightly at the corners. She didn't want anything touching her. Not the chair or her clothes or anything else. Even her skin had begun to hurt.

She breathed through the silence in the room, surviving in four-second intervals that she counted as she exhaled.

"I have pills and an injection." Trey returned holding a surprisingly professional looking medical kit. "Which do you want?"

"Injection. Two injections. Stick it in my eyeball, I don't care. Whatever will work fastest." She ground her teeth together.

Trey administered the injection, then sat on the coffee table in front of her. He didn't ask if she was doing okay, or bother her with any other words, which would only have ripped away the little bit of perseverance she had left. He just sat, watchful and serious.

Thank the ancient gods for him. She'd leave an offering or something if she believed in that stuff. But she did believe in him.

The pain lessened in tiny increments, like a knot being pried loose with great effort. When she was able to relax her arms and lean against the back of the chair, she sighed with relief. She still hurt, but she no longer felt like she wanted to crawl out of her own skin.

"Thanks," she said, without elaborating on what she was thankful for. They both knew and there was no reason to belabor it. "I'm going to stay here for a few minutes, then use the san unit. Why don't you look around and take inventory?"

"Sure. Yell if you need anything." He stood and went

to the kitchenette to begin his survey.

She needed to pee, take a hot shower, eat a bowl of Aunt Ruth's chicken soup, and down a glass of whiskey. She was only going to get a couple of those things, and even those would have to wait until the painkiller was working a little better.

Finally, Reece heaved herself to her feet and shuffled off to the bathroom.

She hoped tomorrow would be a better day.

Much better.

* * * * *

Reece woke up to a darkened room, a pillow under her head, and a really ripping hangover.

The pillow she hadn't had, last she knew, so Trey must have provided that. Nice of him. And since he hadn't let her have any whiskey last night, the hangover wasn't from that, but rather a result of the aftereffects of the medication.

She steeled herself before undertaking the effort of moving her body into a sitting position.

Okay. She could do this.

She dragged herself upright, and it actually wasn't too bad. A little tired and discombobulated, but only a few minor aches. Not much worse than she'd expect from sleeping on the couch.

After a shower and a change into some baggy shorts and a soft shirt, she felt almost human again. A cup of coffee should get her the rest of the way there. And then she could get to work.

She had a lot to do.

Tiptoeing to the kitchen to avoid waking Trey, she brewed a pot of coffee and made some toast while she waited for the black joy. She didn't have an appetite, but she needed to eat to get back to her regular self.

By the time Trey got up an hour later, Reece had coffee, eaten toast, and felt like at least seventy percent of her normal self.

Which was more than enough to kick a whole lot of ass.

"How are you?" Trey asked, his voice rough with sleep.

She got up and poured him a cup of coffee. To repay him for looking after her, she'd kept some brewed and warm for him. "Like someone who was recently brought back from the dead, but doing better."

"I guess that's encouraging, then?" He accepted the cup of coffee from her and took a long drink from it.

Reece shrugged. "It's something. At least, it's enough for us to get back to work."

He gave her a crooked, sleepy smile. "For the people who just cut us loose and are probably trying to hunt us down for who knows what purpose?"

"Hah. Not that kind of work. Similar concept, but in this case, it's more about survival than a paycheck. Same basic tactics, though."

"Well, there we go. Job's half done already, then."

She arched an eyebrow at him. "How do you figure that?"

"Because you're the best at your job, and I'm currently second best."

"Currently?"

He looked smug. "I don't do anything that I don't plan to become the best at."

She rolled her eyes, smiling. "Great. If you're so smart, and so close to eclipsing me, what's our next move?"

"I didn't say I was close. Just that it's inevitable. But since you asked…" he pursed his lips thoughtfully. "First priority is finding Schramm, obviously. But since he's been unseen for a while, we'll probably have to go at it in a roundabout way. Figuring out what happened to Erving would probably lead us in the right direction."

"Is that what you're going with?"

He frowned. "Should I change my answer?"

"Only if you think you should."

After a moment, he shook his head. "No, that's the direction I'd go. But I'm sure, with all your experience and wisdom and yadda-yadda, you have a much more ingenious idea."

"Not really," she said with the hint of a smile. "Tracking Erving was my first thought, too. Wherever he went, whether we actually find Erving or not, we'll get some answers."

Trey slapped the table, making her blink. "Look there, I got one right."

He was humoring her again. She was sure of it.

She pretended not to notice. "Presumably, Erving would have been at his apartment before coming to meet us. We can figure his most-likely route from his place to the Debtor's Haven, then check security cameras and whatnot to see what we can find. If he never even attempted to get there, we'll know he either fled or was grabbed beforehand."

"That sounds like a big job," Trey said. "How do we get access to those cameras?"

"Corporate ones, we can't. But private ones are fair game. Most businesses employ someone to handle the cameras and the security monitoring for them. It's a pretty regional system because it makes sense to use the same surveillance company that your neighbors do, to provide overlap. So, once we get Erving's home address, we can figure out who works that area, and pay that person a visit."

Trey sat and set his cup on the table. "I like it. But, uh..." He looked away, not meeting Reece's gaze.

"What?"

"I mean...is that what you're going to wear? Because..." Trey's face revealed a special mix of discomfort and disapproval.

She threw her napkin at him and got up. "My clothes are in the wash. They'll be done in a few minutes, probably."

He caught the napkin. "Well, then we're all set."

It wasn't like he was dressed up and looking cool. He wore a pair of shorts that were too tight and that was it. Tommy clearly hadn't equipped the safehouse with someone of Trey's size in mind.

But had she said anything? Made remarks about his hairy chest or how his shorts made his...ugh. No. She didn't even want to think about what she hadn't said. She wanted to go on pretending she hadn't seen what she hadn't talked about.

* * * * *

"Got it." Reece hadn't needed much time to figure out who handled the security footage of Erving's neighborhood. "We need to go see Apolla."

"Is this someone you know?" Trey, thankfully, had dressed in his usual clothes, which left a great deal more to the imagination.

"Eh."

"Eh?" he repeated. "I find this an insufficient response. Try again."

"We're acquainted. We move in circles that overlap a bit. She's not corporate."

"Is that good, or bad?"

"Neither. It just is what it is. If she were corporate, I might be able to pull some strings via mutual acquaintances—you know, the old friend-of-a-friend deal. But she's like Tommy, entirely private. That means we'll have to find what she cares about and bargain with that. Let's do some research on her before we drop in."

"We're not going to make an appointment, I take it?" he asked.

"If we ask beforehand, she could say no, or disappear. That won't happen if we just show up."

He nodded, but his attention had shifted. Reece could see from the tiny, sharp movements of his eyes that he'd already begun running queries via his Link.

Sometimes she wondered what his interface looked like. Was it more sophisticated than hers, due to the technological difference between her people and his?

She'd never know because it was literally all inside his head.

An hour later they were in an autotaxi, headed for the metro station. From there they'd go straight to Apolla's place of work, which was also her place of residence, located just outside the downtown commercial area.

The location alone told Reece something about Apolla. If she were flush with cash or eager to appear as if she were, she'd live right in the downtown district. The fact that she lived just outside it said that she either couldn't afford it or didn't care what people thought.

Reece wondered which one of those two options it was.

Rather than sleeping during the trip, she made use of every minute, tracking down every single mention of Apolla she could find, just in case it shed further light on the security tech's character.

When they pulled up outside the building, Reece took a moment to close her eyes for a bit before exiting the taxi.

They took the stairs up to avoid the camera in the building's elevator. Not all buildings had one, but of course this one did. The stairwell, like most, didn't have them though, due to the fact that it would take a lot of them to adequately monitor the area, and good security equipment wasn't cheap. Besides, nobody used stairwells in tall buildings when there were perfectly good elevators available. Monitoring stairwells in a residence just wasn't worth the cost.

Trey put a hand on Reece's elbow, causing her to stop before she began climbing up. "Something keeps bothering me. Are you sure this is the right course of action? I mean, I see that you're loyal to Schramm, but is he loyal to you? What if he's in on whatever's going on? I need to know that you're really sure we aren't better off just getting outsystem, at least for now."

Reece paused. "I get what you're saying. And you might be right. The thing about loyalty is that you can't be truly, completely certain about it until it's stressed in a tough situation. As far as I'm concerned, this is my big test, and I'm going to pass it. I won't know about Schramm until we see how it all turns out."

He searched her face, then nodded. "That's how I had it figured, too, but I would have been remiss if I hadn't mentioned it."

"You would have," she agreed, starting up the stairs.

"So I did."

"Yes. I know. Good job."

He climbed the stairs alongside her. "Is that a genuine 'good job,' or are you being condescending toward me?"

"Condescending. Actually, no. It's both."

"How can it be both?"

"It just is."

Trey was silent for a couple of flights, then he said, "You're a little too comfortable with ambiguity, I think."

"Am I? What have absolutes ever done for me?" Reece checked the floor number. Two more to go. Good thing they were getting close, because she still didn't feel entirely well yet.

"Probably about as much as they've done for me," Trey replied as he pushed open the door on the fifth floor and she followed.

They arrived at the apartment and Reece wished they had a clever plan to get inside, but Trey simply pushed the doorbell. If Apolla didn't let them in, they'd just break in. One way or the other, they'd get in there in the quickest way available to them.

"Yes?" A voice asked.

"This is Reece, from Rexcare. I was hoping you could help me with something."

"Business or personal?"

Reece hesitated. Which one of those would be the right category? "Some of both," she said.

A moment later the door opened, a young woman standing before them, looking guarded but curious. "Why didn't you make an appointment?"

"I was afraid you'd say no," Reece said.

Apolla smiled. She had dark eyes and dark skin and looked even younger when she smiled. Her records had indicated she was only twenty. Very young for someone to be as successful and well-known as she was.

"I like honesty. Come in." She stepped back.

Reece hadn't had to lie, cheat, or shoot her way in. She liked this refreshing change of pace. She noted details of the room as she entered. Unlike most apartments, this one opened into a small foyer that apparently doubled as a sitting room. At the back, a doorway on either side led to other rooms.

Apolla motioned to the uncomfortable-looking straight-backed chairs. "This is where I see people. Sorry the furniture isn't fancier. My dumbass brother broke it, and all the good stuff needed a couple weeks for delivery."

Reece was beginning to like Apolla. "How did he break it?"

Apolla sighed. "He's seventeen. He watched a sim where a guy jumped off a balcony to chase down some thieves. My brother wanted to see what that would be like. And then I got to see what it was like to come home to a smashed table and two broken chairs. Like I said, he's a dumbass."

Trey grinned. "Sounds about right for that age."

Apolla raised her eyebrows at him. "You sound like you speak from experience."

"Oh, yeah. I did dumb crap too when I was younger. Don't worry, he'll grow out of it. Mostly. Eventually." He looked regretful. "Actually, it could take a while."

"Great." Apolla sighed and sank to one of the chairs, then grimaced. "These chairs are like sitting on a metallic cactus."

Trey had begun to sit, but he straightened. "Damn. I think I'll stand."

If one of them didn't sit, it would be awkward, so it was up to Reece. But how bad could it be? Surely Apolla was exaggerating. The seat looked flat and rigid, but not at all pointy.

She sat. "Oh. Oh you're right. This really sucks."

Apolla laughed. "Yep. Anyway, what did you two need? The sooner we discuss it, the sooner you can stop sitting there."

Trey, leaning against a wall, said, "We were supposed to meet someone, but he didn't show. And he hasn't shown up anywhere, since, so far as we can tell. We'd like to check security footage and see if we can figure out where he's gone."

Apolla's expression became guarded. "This sounds like a civil issue. I don't do that. You end up making enemies that way."

Reece shook her head. "He's a colleague. "

"So this is official Rexcare business? You said it was both business and personal."

"Rexcare won't look into it. Or at least if they do, they won't tell me what they found. And I need to know, which is what makes it personal."

Apolla fixed Reece with a long, steady look. "If they're not looking into it, there's a reason. Is he expendable to them?"

"I'm not sure," Reece admitted. "He does important work, but how much the company values that, I don't know."

Apolla sighed. "You're a fixer. Why would you come to me for help?"

"To fix it. I work with a lot of people in the private sector, both officially and unofficially. Whatever it takes to get the job done. That's what being a fixer is."

Apolla stared at her. "Let me ask this: If I agreed to help you, who would my employer be? You, or Rexcare?"

Ah, this one was smart. That was both good and bad. Good because she'd have valuable skills and brainpower, and bad because she'd be a lot harder to mislead.

"Us, technically. But that's normal for something that someone wants to keep quiet. I'm sure you've heard that."

The general public was far from unaware of how wide-ranging a fixer's job duties could be.

Apolla shook her head slowly. "I have to admit, I can't tell if you're being genuine, or selling a cartload a crap. What I'm sure of is that there's someone you want to find, and you don't want to leave a trail in doing finding him. But I'm not in the people-finding business. I do surveillance work. That's it."

"So you won't help us?" Trey asked.

"I *will* help you," Apolla said.

"Why?" Reece hadn't figured this young woman out yet.

"Because I'm ambitious. Because I'm good at what I do. Because I think you really do want to find someone and not for a bad reason. And because I need to buy a new table and chairs." Apolla stood up, rubbing her behind. "My ass hurts."

Reece and Trey laughed.

"But," Apolla said pointedly, holding up a finger for emphasis, "there are things I won't do. So if I say no, that's it. And if I get the feeling you're doing something wrong or misleading me, I will do my best to make things go terribly wrong for you."

"I like how you told us that up front," Trey said. "It shows foresight."

Apolla smirked at him. "Come on back to my office."

Trey straightened and pulled away from the wall. "We're going to look right now?"

"The way I understand missing people," Apolla said, "the longer they're gone, the less likely they are to turn up, right? The trail gets cold fast."

Reece nodded.

"Plus," Apolla went on, "my office chairs are much nicer."

* * * * *

Reece and Trey spent ten minutes describing Erving, his position at Rexcare, and what time he failed to show up to meet them.

Apolla made notes, nodding and looking thoughtful. "You've got the time nailed down really well, and given the time of the meeting, there's a defined radius for how far away he could have been during that time. I'll plot that out, see how much of it lands in my zone and how much, if any, lands in someone else's. Then I'll look at the feeds that seem most likely to have something and go from there."

"How long do you think it will take? Reece asked.

"Depends. I might find something right away, or I might have to get footage from someone else. That's usually not a problem, since it's something my colleagues and I do on a regular basis, but it takes time to get it and go through it. It could be anywhere from an hour to a day."

A day at the longest was impressive. Reece only hoped Erving didn't slip out of reach during that time. "You'll contact me as soon as you have anything?"

Apolla nodded. "Of course. I find it interesting that you haven't yet asked what this is going to cost."

"I find it interesting that you haven't yet told me what it'll cost," Reece countered.

Apolla smiled faintly. "Let's say a hundred credits an hour base rate, with the option to adjust if something unexpected comes up."

It was reasonable for the service, but Reece didn't like the idea of an adjustment.

"Let's say two hundred an hour, plus expenses incurred," Reece said.

Apolla looked from Reece to Trey, remaining silent for a long moment. Finally, she said, "Agreed."

Reece and Trey left so Apolla could get right to work. In the stairwell on the way back down, Trey asked, "Are you sure we shouldn't have asked her to look for Schramm? In addition to, or instead of, Erving?"

"He's too important. If I named him as missing, she'd know something big was up, and would either take information to someone who could pay more for it than I can, or leak the information to someone who could use it. Then Schramm would be compromised."

They reached ground level and went outside into the heat. Was it Reece's imagination or did it seem maybe a degree cooler today? Might they have finally gotten over the peak of the perihelion? She checked the date. Yeah. It seemed they had. Not that one degree was enough to get excited about. But knowing that the temperature would gradually go down over the next couple of months sounded grand to her.

"What now, then?" Trey asked.

She'd been wondering the same thing, herself. Should they go back to the safehouse, to stay out of view, or hang around in the vicinity, in case Apolla turned up something quickly?

Trey put a hand on her shoulder. "Let's get some food. You're still not back to normal."

"We shouldn't be out in public."

"We'll go someplace too crappy to have cameras," he said. "And I'll buy you a hat."

"I don't look good in hats."

"That would only make it an even better disguise."

"No one wears hats in this weather," she pointed out. "I'd stand out because of the hat."

"Oh. Well, that makes sense. What about lightshade glasses?"

"Very common."

"Then I'll get you lightshade glasses." He sounded pleased with himself. "And buy you a crappy lunch."

"Sadly, that's the best offer I've had for a while, so I guess I'll have to take it." She tried not to think about that too hard, because it might bum her out.

"That's the spirit." He patted her shoulder before letting his arm drop.

She looked right and left, deciding which way they could more easily duck cameras.

Trey nodded to the left. "Let's go that way. There's a crappy ramen place over there."

True to his word, he bought her a pair of oversized lightshade glasses, along with a summer headscarf.

"Look what I found!" He seemed very happy when he came out. "I've seen women wearing these. You can pull your hair into a bun with it and hide your skin from the these burning orbs in your sky."

"A bun? That's not my style." Reece frowned at the pale yellow fabric in her hand. It was so light it felt weightless.

"Exactly." He put a pair of lightshade glasses on.

"If I wear this, then you have to wear one too," Reece countered.

"I don't have enough hair for a bun."

She rolled her eyes. "Obviously. But men wear scarves too. The styling's different, is all. Women tuck it around their faces and sometimes their hair, but men just drape it over their heads and let the ends hang down the front. One second, I'll get you one."

She went into the little bodega he'd visited. She had a moment of indecision on color, but she chose a style she thought would really suit him.

"Here." She handed it to him as soon as she exited the bodega.

He looked down at the airy fabric she'd put in his hand. "It's purple. And it has pineapples on it."

She blinked innocently. "I thought you'd like the pineapple thing. And it's not purple. It's lavender."

"Well, yeah. The pineapples are good. I just never saw myself as a lavender kind of guy."

"Exactly," she said, copying his tone of voice from when he'd said the word. "All the better for the disguise, right?"

"Well...I guess. And it does have pineapples." He draped the fabric over his head, arranging the ends in front of his shoulders.

After they'd walked for a couple of minutes, Trey made a thoughtful sound. "Huh. I thought this thing would make my head hot, but it actually feels cooler."

"It's the fabric. Specially designed for UV protection

and cooling. Emergency kits often have them to help cool people off."

"How did I not know about this?" he asked in wonder. "I need, like, a hundred of these."

She laughed. "I'm glad you like it."

"Wait." He stopped to look at her full-face. "Do they make blankets out of this stuff?"

"Yeah, but they're only used for medical care. Treating for heat stroke or fever or whatever."

"I'm going to get one to sleep in! I'm always get hot and sweaty when I sleep, even in a cool room. This is going to be awesome!" He did a little hop, then started walking again.

He seemed so genuinely delighted that she laughed. He was like a little kid receiving solstice presents.

They turned down a side alley to avoid an intersection with cameras.

"Hey, here's a question for you," Trey began.

"Okay."

"Can we talk about the fact that your weapons dealer is equipped with sedatives and paralytics?"

"Sure," she agreed. "What about it."

"Well, where I come from, anyone would find that a deeply disturbing turn of events. But you don't?"

"Eh. Nah."

"Why not?" he asked, sounding terribly curious.

"Simple. Because he's on my side. I mean, if he weren't, sure, that would be some screwed up stuff, but..." she shrugged.

"Huh. Well...okay, then. I guess." He didn't sound entirely convinced, but although he was adapting well to life on Akon, he still had things to learn about how its citizens approached life.

They returned to the main street and Trey paused, looking in each direction.

Reece tensed. "What's wrong? Did you see something?"

"No. I just can't remember if the place is one block down or one block up. I didn't travel by alleyway last time I was here."

"What's the name? We can check the address on the Link."

"I don't think it had one."

She squinted at him. "All restaurants have a name. It's a business. It has to register as something."

"Well, then I missed it."

"Okay. Let's walk back a block, then walk back up if we don't see it. Or we could find something else. Or just go back to the safehouse. I'm feeling better, actually. I think all that stair climbing helped work out the stiffness."

"It's really good ramen. Let's see if we can find it." Barely ten steps later, he stopped. "That's it! See? It doesn't have a name."

Reece laughed. She pointed at flowing script painted top to bottom on the front of the building. "It says 'Marigold' right here."

"What, those squiggles? I thought that was a design."

"Nah, it's an old writing style no one uses, except for stylized things like this."

"So why can you read it?" he asked.

"I wouldn't be much of a fixer if I couldn't read

anything that might be written on Akon." She blinked, realizing what she'd just said. "Uh, I didn't mean…"

"Yeah. I know. I'll just have to learn to read this script, that's all."

"I'll teach you," she offered as they ducked under a low archway to the entrance of the little hole-in-the-wall restaurant.

Trey laughed. "No way."

"Why not?"

"You don't strike me as the kind and patient teacher type. I'll do self-study via the Link or hire someone to teach me after we get all this stuff sorted."

He made it sound like they just needed to do some minor yardwork, not do battle with one of the biggest corporations in the system.

"Well, I offered." She tried not to be offended that he'd turn that offer down.

"Believe me," he said, "I'm saving us both a lot of headache. And possibly our partnership as well."

They sat at a table, facing each other, which gave her the perfect opportunity to gaze at him in exasperation. "I'm not that bad."

"You are. You're pushy, demanding, and kind of a jerk sometimes. But I'm good with that. I actually like those things about you. They just don't make for a good teacher, just not for me. Okay?"

Put that way, it didn't sound like so much fun to Reece. She shrugged.

Trey grinned at her. "Aww, did I hurt your feelings?"

She sighed. "No."

"Yes, I did. I hurt your cute widdle feelings."

"If you don't promise never to do that baby talk thing that you just did, ever again, I'll have to kill you in your sleep." She glared at him.

"See? Told ya you were a jerk."

The server arrived, saving Reece from having to come back with a really crushing response. Frankly, she didn't have one, and it would have hurt her pride to admit it.

Yeah, Trey was right. She was kind of a jerk sometimes. But so was he.

"What's popular?" Reece asked the server, an older woman with a pleasant smile.

"Everything. But our biggest sellers are the mushroom ramen and the Ruffino chili."

"Mushroom sounds good. I'll try that." Reece took a deep breath, savoring the fantastic smell. If it was any indicator, the food would be as good as Trey said.

"I'll take the chili one," Trey decided.

"That one's spicy," the woman said.

"I like spicy," he assured her.

"Very good. I'll get these orders in. It shouldn't take too long."

She wasn't kidding. What seemed like just a few minutes later, steaming bowls of food arrived at their table, emitting ridiculously appetizing aromas of onion, vegetables, chilis, among others.

They dug in with delight. Within a couple of minutes, though, Trey began wiping his forehead.

"Something wrong?" she asked.

He wiped his forehead again and squirmed.

"No, I'm fine." He took a long drink of tea.

"You're sweating."

"She wasn't kidding about this being hot." He sniffed. "It's really good though."

"Do you want to switch?" She pointed at her bowl.

"Only if you're cool with scorching your insides. I'm trying to play it cool here, but truth is, I'm pretty sure I'm dissolving from the inside out."

She laughed and switched their bowls. "It's fine. Akon spice has no equal that I know of. We have pernicious peppers that we actually use for pest control. We have spicy tomatoes and squash, and even a variety of spicy apple. We have some very unique crops."

He watched her, and she realized he was waiting for her to take a bite.

She scooped some up and slurped it down. A ball of flame formed in her mouth. She blew out a breath. "Yep. That's hot all right."

She took another bite.

He shrugged and began eating the mushroom ramen. She was pretty sure she heard him let out a small sigh of relief.

She hid her amusement for his sake. It felt like the thing to do.

As she was sipping the last of the broth from her bowl, a message alert came up on the left side of her vision. That was interesting, since she'd squelched everything except for her closest contacts.

She accessed the message, which was a brief text, and set her bowl down. Then she picked it back up and drained it of the last dregs of broth because doing otherwise would no doubt end up being a regret somewhere down the line. It was too delicious to waste.

"Done?" she asked Trey.

He narrowed his eyes at her. "No. But why do I get the feeling you know something I don't?"

"Our new friend just left me a message. She's got something."

He tilted his head back and, with astonishing ease, downed the remainder of his ramen—noodles, mushrooms, and all, with one long pour.

She'd never been so impressed with him.

Trey pushed back from the table. "Let's go."

EYES EVERYWHERE
DATE: 05.25.8948 (Adjusted Gregorian)
LOCATION: Apolla's Appartment, Ohiyo, Akonwara
REGION: Machete System, PED 4B, Orion Freedom Alliance

"I like that you found something so fast," Trey said, standing in Apolla's entry room. "This bodes well."

"Don't get too excited." Apolla seemed oddly reserved for someone who had managed to be successful in a very short amount of time.

Reece doubted that it boded *entirely* well for them.

Apolla beckoned them forward and led them to her work area. She took her sim out of rest mode and gestured at the images on display. "There. See?"

Reece wasn't sure she did. She squinted at the images, which were mostly blurs and shadows to her eyes. "Why don't you give us your professional opinion?"

Apolla began manipulating two 3D sims at the same time, spinning them around. One, she arranged from the top down, and the other, she spun into a straight-on view of what looked like a hallway corridor.

"This is your guy." She pointed at the hallway view. "He's leaving his apartment right at the time you indicated. No doubt on his way to see you. But check this out."

She made a gesture with her hands and the top-down view illuminated with night vision, showing a street view with one person in it. She activated it, and it showed Erving walking toward a taxi. Then two people came in quickly from out of frame and shoved Erving into a different vehicle, their actions quick and efficient.

"Well, that's not good," Reece observed. "Can you get detailed visuals on the faces of his abductors?"

Apolla looked over her shoulder at Reece and smirked. "Of course, I can. I see *everything* that happens under my cameras."

Apolla rolled the footage back, then reached out to the sim and flexed her fingers. She bent them then pulled her wrists back, and the view expanded, but didn't lose clarity. In fact, somehow, the detail increased.

Yeah, Apolla was good at her job. Damn good.

How had Reece not discovered her before? She'd have been helpful in other cases Reece had worked.

"Mapping the faces and running them against the registered database," Apolla muttered.

After a couple of tense minutes, Apolla said "Got 'em." Then her tone changed and she added, "Well, that's weird."

Reece and Trey exchanged a glance. Whatever Apolla was seeing, it didn't seem to be a good thing.

"Those two are low-level thugs for Pritney-Dax," Apolla said. "Any idea why they'd want to abduct the assistant of a top-level exec of arguably the biggest corporation in Machete?"

"No," Reece admitted. "Declaring war on Rexcare by abducting a critical employee is out of Pritney-Dax's league. And abducting an executive assistant just isn't done. Critical or not, no one's going to pay a ransom for him. It doesn't make sense."

Apolla shook her head and rotated her chair around to face Reece and Trey. "That's what I thought. So, you two have a mystery on your hands."

"Yeah," Reece said. "Looks like it. Can you see if you can tell exactly where these guys were before abducting Erving?"

"Is that a bigger priority than seeing where they went afterward?" Apolla asked.

"No. That's second priority. Let me know as soon as you have any idea where they've taken Erving, and you can tell me whatever you come up with via the Link."

Apolla paused. "Is that wise? Your company could be listening."

Right. It wouldn't be the greatest idea to let Apolla know that Reece had jailbroken her hardware. "I meant via Trey. His Link wasn't paid for by Rexcare, so it's clean."

Apolla nodded. "Understood. And since I have a feeling you aren't going to just go plant posies in the garden while you wait to hear from me, let me know if you turn up anything that could be useful, okay? If they've left my zone—and there's a good chance of that—I'll have to reach out to colleagues to track them. Any hints about what district they could have gone to would save time."

"Of course," Reece said. "Good luck."

"You too," Apolla said. "Seems like you'll need it. You two can let yourselves out. I have a lot to do."

When they got out to the hallway, Trey said, "I'll contact her while we walk down."

"Who?" Reece asked.

"Raya. We both know that Pritney-Dax's primary fixer is Shepherd, and that you've never been nice to him. Raya has a much better relationship with him, and therefore, if we want his help, we need her help to get it."

They entered stairwell and Reece eyed him for a moment before beginning the descent. "Well done. Pretty soon, you won't need me at all."

"Sure, but I'll keep you around anyway, for morale." He nudged her with his elbow gently.

She jabbed back, not so gently. "So, what does Raya say? When can she meet?"

"It's been fifteen seconds! Relax."

"What a stupid thing to say. We're on the run and our boss and his assistant are missing. How am I supposed to relax?"

He sighed. "What I meant was that you need to be patient."

"I can be patient if I have to. Relaxed, not so much."

"Tell me about it," he muttered so quietly that she almost didn't catch it.

She couldn't disagree with him. Their recent beach trip notwithstanding, she did have difficulty relaxing, generally speaking. "So what does she say?"

"Augh! Can you give me at least two full minutes to observe the usual greeting, asking how she is, and *then* requesting her help?"

"If I have to. But I won't like it." She began counting the stairs as they walked down them, estimating that she took two of them for every second.

By the time they reached the landing to the second floor, she was sure two minutes had passed. "Well?"

"She'll meet us. I told her we should stay out of

camera view whenever possible, and she said we could go to the urban park on the northeast side and meet her by the pond."

"Good. I'll call a taxi." Reece sent an alert for one to be sent to the building and when they exited a couple minutes later, a taxi was already waiting.

Reece hurried through the heat to slide into the vehicle.

She gave the driver their destination and off they went. She guessed they were only about ten minutes from their destination, so she stayed awake, watching the city go by outside her window.

<So what do you think?> Trey asked her via the Link.

<Nothing yet.>

<Really? I thought you might already have the whole scenario figured out, with all of your expertise.>

<I'm good at my job. Not psychic. There's a difference.>

He turned his head to give her a sad look. <Can't say I'm not disappointed. You could have at least maintained the illusion of being psychic, just for my sake.>

<Why would you want me to do that?>

<Everyone needs to have something special to believe in.>

She gave him her best you're-an-idiot expression, then pointedly turned her head toward the window so she couldn't see him.

Instead, she focused her attention on meeting with Raya. How could they best secure her help? The offer of money, or using Trey's budding relationship with her?

Probably a mix of both, but since he didn't talk about Raya much, Reece would have to try to gauge their relationship based on their behavior when they were all together.

She thought about it all the way to the park, and right up until she saw Raya. Reece had to wonder where she'd been that she could arrive at the park before them.

Hanging back, she let Trey approach Raya first. They gave each other a casual, beside-the-mouth greeting kiss that was personal but not intimate. It was the kind of smooch family members gave one another, or longtime friends, making it an inconclusive indicator of the intensity of their relationship.

Raya moved in and gave Reece the same beside-the-mouth smooch, taking her by surprise.

Raya grinned. "We meet again, under shady circumstances."

"Why do you assume they're shady."

Raya waved at the trees overhead. "Shade. Ha ha. You're way too serious."

"You would be, too, if your company had burned you."

Raya's eyes widened. "What? Come sit. Tell me everything."

Reece and Trey laid it out to her, relaying the facts quickly, while not mentioning Apolla's name. Chances were, Raya already knew of her, but Reece didn't see any reason to stick Apolla into all this. Besides, Reece hoped to make an asset of Apolla in the future and didn't want to share her with Raya.

"So you want me to butter Shepherd up and find out about the thugs that abducted Erving?"

"That about covers it," Trey agreed. "We can get you their faces, in case you need them."

"I'm sure if they work for Pritney-Dax, Shepherd will know them, but what if he doesn't want to tell me? What should I offer him?"

"If you can't get by on sheer charm alone, which I doubt," Reece said, "you'll have to offer him something he'd want. So what would he want?"

"A job at Rexcare or Donnercorp," Raya answered promptly.

The thought of having to work in the same company with Shepherd made Reece's guts turn to ice. She might never get her job back at Rexcare, but she wanted to maintain the possibility of going back. "Okay, offer him a job at Donnercorp."

Raya laughed. "No way. Not even if I needed the information for myself."

"Then we'll need something else," Trey said.

"We could owe him a favor," Reece said reluctantly.

"What 'we'?" Raya asked. "You and Trey kind of 'we', or the kind of 'we' that involves me, too?"

"Either. Both. Whatever gets the identity of those two guys."

Raya sighed. "Fine. But you'll owe me a favor."

"What kind of 'you' is that?" Trey asked. "The kind that's just Reece, or the kind that involves me, too?"

Raya laughed at his repeating her words. "Let's talk about it over dinner tonight."

Reece opened her mouth but Raya cut her off.

"Just him." Raya smiled. "Don't worry," she said to Trey. "I'll keep you out of sight."

Trey sent Reece a questioning look.

Reece nodded. "No reason not to, so long as you're

careful. I'll stay holed up at the safehouse."

Trey looked surprised. "I expected you to say something about there being no time for dating under these circumstances."

"The way I figure it," Reece said, "if you and Raya can't handle whatever you might come up against, we're screwed anyway."

"Hadn't thought of it that way." Trey scratched his chin. "But it makes sense."

Raya nodded. "Okay. I'll go see Shepherd, meet Trey for dinner tonight, and then we'll see what we know at that point."

"Let us know right away if you get names," Reece said.

"And if your surveillance person comes up with more, let me know about that," Raya answered.

Reece nodded.

"As much as I hate to leave, I'm sure you want me to get right on this. Besides, if I sweat any more, I'm going to need to change before I can go to Pritney-Dax." Raya put her hand on Trey's arm for a moment, then strode away.

Trey watched her go, obviously enjoying the view.

Reece nudged him. "Besides a perfect face, legs a kilometer long, and a great personality, what do you see in her?"

Trey grinned at her. "You like to pretend you're jealous of her, but you're not."

"Who says?" Reece challenged.

"You aren't that hung up on your looks, or on what people think of you. You don't need that stuff."

She didn't know whether to be pleased or disturbed that he'd come to understand her so well. "Let's go before I melt."

"Want to grab some container-ice on the way back to the safehouse?" he asked. "I noticed it was the one thing Tommy hadn't thought to stock up on."

"That's an emphatic yes. Let's go!"

* * * * *

While Trey was out on his date, and Apolla was looking for information, Reece had nothing to do.

Literally nothing. The safehouse didn't even have a place to work out. It did have a sim, so she switched on one of Aunt Ruth's game shows and got a container-ice.

She sat down, cracked the package, and gave it a few seconds to freeze over. Then she opened it and took a bite.

Raspberry. Yum.

It wasn't so bad, she supposed, having some down time. She definitely didn't mind the privacy. It felt a little weird not even having Dex around, though.

Nah. She'd rather be out getting the job done. She could work on the "going with the flow" thing when she no longer had concerns about her company trying to make her disappear. Or whatever it was they were doing.

Too bad they would have cut off her access to Rexcare's systems right away.

Actually. She jerked herself upright and dropped her container-ice on the table. They would have cut off the access they knew about.

Without a doubt, they had blocked the registered accounts for Reece and Trey. But Trey had recently been a new employee, and new employees had provisional access until their entire employment package was processed. Since corporations tended to be slow with paperwork, and departments didn't always communicate that well, Trey's provisional account might still work.

Holding her breath, she activated her Link and connected to Rexcare's front end system, manually entered Trey's provisional access token, and waited.

It worked.

She blinked in surprise, then cackled like a lunatic. Immediately, she looked up the company's official roster. Yep. There Schramm was in his rightful place as chief officer. There were only two people in the company with as much power, and two with almost as much.

Were those four her main suspects? If Schramm had been forced to go on the run, only an order from above him would have caused him to take such drastic steps. Which begged the question: who could, and would, do that?

Of course, this was assuming Schramm hadn't done something to bring this on himself. Reece had to consider that possibility too. And she did—for about fifteen seconds. Then she discarded it. Schramm lived for his job, and he lived for the company. He wouldn't do anything contrary to company interests.

That brought her back to who would want him out of Rexcare.

The other top two execs could do it. Tillson and Jono.

Would they, though? Probably. In the right situation. But what would that situation be?

The other possibility was the head of the board of the directors, Janice. Her job didn't involve running the company, but rather keeping the company's officers accountable to the shareholders. She often had a contentious relationship with Rexcare's officers, but mostly she got along with them quite well. Usually, it depended on how the company was doing financially at the time.

If Reece limited her searches to Tillson, Jono, and Janice, she might come up with a most likely candidate. Or she might simply have more background information when Apolla got back to her. Or when Raya got something useful out of Shepherd.

Information was good. Reece couldn't have too much of it at this point.

She didn't have access to the deeper, more secretive stuff her own account would have provided, but she was able to see the recent schedules of the three, the meetings they'd taken, and the minutes of recent board meetings.

Reece didn't usually pay much attention to that kind of stuff because it was too top-end to have any relevance to her. She was as bottom-side at Rexcare as it got. Heck, it was sometimes her job to get extra dirty just to save Rexcare from having knowledge or contact with something that could be harmful.

After a few hours of reading, she felt she had a good handle on the current state of affairs at the top ranks. She knew that Tillson and Jono wanted to invest heavily into research while Janice wanted them to focus on optimizing profits on existing assets. She didn't see any particularly contentious points between Schramm and anyone.

That fit with her understanding of the man. He was someone who put his shoulder into work and pushed hard, not someone who did things for personal aggrandizement. He was cool and methodical.

So why would someone want him out of the way?

Reece didn't know. Yet. But she felt better prepared to figure it out.

She showered and got ready for bed, enjoying the silence of the safehouse. Wherever Schramm was, she hoped he was safe, too.

VISITORS
DATE: 05.26.8948 (Adjusted Gregorian)
LOCATION: Tommy's Safehouse, near Ohiyo, Akonwara
REGION: Machete System, PED 4B, Orion Freedom Alliance

Reece woke to the sound of a crash. She leaped out of bed, grabbed her Rikulfs and bolted toward the door.

And heard Trey cursing and eased into the hall which led toward the safehouse's kitchen. Slowing, she entered, and flipped on a light.

Trey jumped back at the sight of Reece. "Whoa! Point those somewhere else." He righted the chair he'd knocked over. "Did I wake you?"

She swallowed a sarcastic reply. "Yeah. How was the date?"

"Nice. Raya's fun."

"She is. Has she found anything out?"

"She talked to Shepherd. He doesn't know the two. He said he can find out, though."

"Quietly, I hope." Reece didn't like the guy, but didn't want him getting into something nasty on their behalf.

"Raya seemed confident in his abilities."

She said, "I checked out your temporary login to the Rexcare system, and it still worked. I was able to do some reconnaissance on what the day-to-day operations have been. They still have Schramm listed, too, so he hasn't been fired or anything."

"That's very interesting. What made you think to try that temporary login? I haven't used that in months."

She shrugged. "Corporations are slow to process that kind of HR stuff. It's low priority so it gets ignored."

"Well, nice going. I'm guessing you didn't find a smoking gun."

She looked down at her Rikulfs, which she held at her sides because she was wearing pajamas and no weapon belt. "Nope. Just these when a big oaf came crashing in. I'm going back to bed. We can talk in the morning unless there was something else."

"Nope. Good night."

"Night."

In her room, Reece returned her pistols to the bedside table. For once, she was glad she hadn't gotten the opportunity to use them.

* * * * *

Violent shaking woke Reece. She didn't know how long she'd been asleep or what time it was, but she was damn certain this was the second time that night she'd been abruptly awakened.

She didn't like it.

She bolt upright to find Trey pressing a finger to his lips. <Someone's outside. One of Tommy's sensors went off.>

Reece slung her belt around her waist and shoved her pistols into it. <Are you sure it's not just an animal?>

<Does an animal say, 'Dammit, Fred, be quiet'?>

<Not in my experience.>

<Then I'd say no.> Trey straightened. <Let's go check the surveillance.>

She moved in that direction but bumped into a

dresser. <*You can see in the dark, right? I don't want to turn anything on in case they notice and clock our position.*>

<*I can't see in complete darkness, but this is okay.*>

She grabbed onto the back of his shirt. <*You lead.*>

Reece shuffled along behind him until they arrived in the other room. The surveillance equipment emitted a small amount of light of their own, so she could see a little. She couldn't make out much on the monitors, though.

<*Two people. Men, I think. On the south side approaching the back door.*>

<*You're running this one,*> Reece whispered in his mind, though she knew it wasn't necessary. <*Tell me what you need.*>

He nodded, leading her to the house's back door. <*They're armed. Not sure with what. Can't tell if it's projectile, energy, or what. I'm going to throw on the flood lights, which should blind them for a few seconds. I'm going to go left. You go right as soon as you're sure you aren't blinded.*>

<*Got it.*> She hoped she and Trey could take them without any killing. She wanted to make them talk.

<*Okay. Now!*> Trey threw on the flood lights.

Reece tilted her head away from the door and the bright lights, then slowly turned it back to see that Trey had already rushed out into the night.

She spared a moment to wish for live surveillance feeds, but Tommy's system didn't allow anyone to log in from the outside and use it via the Link. That was smart from an anti-hacking point of view, but it was a distinct inconvenience at the moment,

Pushing those thoughts from her mind, Reece stepped out into the night, glad that at least now she could see everything. Trey was grappling with one of the intruders and making sure that his opponent's body was between himself and the other guy, who was currently pointing a weapon at the struggling pair while edging closer.

Reece wished she'd had the presence of mind to grab a pulse pistol when Trey had woken her.

Time to put that target practice to good use.

She pulled Righty out of its holster, took careful aim, and squeezed the trigger, hitting the second attacker in the hand. His arm jerked back and his weapon fell to the ground.

Reece didn't give him a chance to recover. She rushed past Trey and the first enemy toward her target. When she got there, the man was holding what was left of his hand, staring at it numbly—then he began to scream.

This presented a conundrum. Reece glanced at Trey to see that he had disarmed his opponent and was sparring with the man.

<Stop playing with your food,> Reece said privately.

<Just getting in some practice. He's not bad. Plus, I don't want to make a huge mess like you did.>

Reece looked back at the man she'd shot. He was under control, but she wanted him shackled. Yet she couldn't exactly cuff his hands behind his back.

On the other hand, he was bleeding quite profusely, and if that didn't stop, he'd soon be no danger to anyone but the people who had to pay for his funeral.

"I'll help you if you help me," she told him. "Do you have any other weapons?"

He pointed to his right leg, his hand shaking.

"Nuh uh, I'm not squatting down there to get it. You'll have to do it. Slowly pull it out, then toss it the other way." She pointed Righty at him.

With a cry that dissolved into a painfully long whimper, the man reached down with his left hand and tossed the knife away.

"Okay." Reece looked over at Trey who seemed to have his opponent well under control. "We're going to walk up to the house, but you're not going inside. All that blood will be murder to get out."

Her choice of words struck her as funny and she laughed.

"Murder to get out. Get it?"

The man looked at her, eyes wide, face pale.

"Guess not. Let's go." She left him standing outside the door while she bolted into the house and grabbed an emergency medical kit.

"Here we go," she said. "You sit down. You're going to pass out any second, and a head wound won't do you any good."

She grabbed him by the armpit of his good arm and the back of his pants. She probably gave him a pretty monster wedgie as she lowered him to the ground, but better his ass than his head.

Grabbing an auto-tourniquet, she stretched it wide to avoid bumping his damaged hand. Actually, it didn't much resemble a hand anymore, but medicine could fix or help most things—short of death.

She let go of the tourniquet and it auto-sized itself around his forearm and began pressurizing. It beeped, then gave a blood pressure reading. It wasn't too awful, all things considered.

The wound stopped gushing.

"There we go. You might just make it, Jack, if you don't do anything stupid." His name almost certainly wasn't Jack, but she had to call him something and he looked like a Jack.

Reece peeled open a sterile wound cover and carefully draped it over the damaged limb. "Okay. That's pretty much all I can do for you. You need a hospital, but you won't die before you get there, so long as you don't wait long enough for infection to set in. I do have a nice injection of painkiller here, and I'll give it to you if you cooperate. Sound like a deal?"

He looked at her, eyes glazed. He was starting to go into shock. Damn. She saw Trey standing over the other guy, talking to him, and hoped he was able to get some answers. She had her doubts about how much help Jack was going to be.

"Okay, let's go with one simple question. That's all. Give me one answer and I'll give you the injection? How's that?"

Jack stared at her.

She continued, "Here's the question: Who are you working for?"

He looked past her, to Trey and the other guy.

"He'll tell us if you don't, but it'd be nice if you two tell the same story." She held the injector up. "Do you have an answer, or should I put this away?"

He quivered. "Apolla."

"Why? Is she working for Pritney-Dax?"

Jack's head drooped and he slumped over. Sighing, Reece caught him by the shoulders and eased him onto his side, making sure he wasn't lying on his injured hand.

Dammit. Things just got more complicated.

* * * * *

"We have to do something with him." Trey frowned at Jack, whose real name was apparently Cliff. It was a common name on Akon—for whatever reason—so she wasn't surprised to have come so close to accurately naming someone off the cuff.

"Yeah, but what? We're trying to stay out of sight, and it's not like we can call a cleanup team from Rexcare." Reece wanted to get the guy to a hospital, but her options were limited.

"Autotaxi?" Trey asked. "Just send him into the city. It'll get stopped, and people will make sure he gets to the hospital. Then we don't have to go anywhere, he gets help, and we can still drill this one's eyeballs out for answers." He jabbed a thumb at the guy he'd apprehended, who now sat, hands behind his back, cuffed to a chair.

Trey's humor really amused Reece sometimes.

She chewed her lip. "I think it's probably the best we can do, in this particular situation. Not ideal, but it ticks all the boxes. Go ahead and call one, but have it come to the end of the road, not to the house. I'll check his vitals and make sure he'll be fine for the trip."

Cliff—formerly known as Jack—was only doing a job

he'd been hired to do. Reece understood that better than anyone, so she didn't take it personally. Besides, no harm had come to her or Trey, and now they had a means of discovering some things they hadn't known before. So really, Cliff had brought her an opportunity.

After they'd packed him into an autotaxi and sent him on his way, they turned their attention to the other guy.

Amusingly, his name turned out to *actually* be Jack. Funny coincidence. It made her wonder if Cliff had thought she'd somehow recognized them and mixed him up with his partner.

Actual Jack had offered his name, then sat quietly while Trey and Reece attended to Cliff. Either Jack cared about his partner's wellbeing or he had no particular reason to argue about giving them his name. He could have simply supplied a false name, but he'd become so compliant that Reece didn't think that was the case.

"Okay, Jack," she said. "There are two ways we can do this."

She'd considered doing a good-guy/bad-guy routine for his benefit, hoping she'd have the chance to be the bad guy, but it didn't seem necessary here. She'd just lay things out for him and he could decide how forthcoming he wanted to be.

He beat her to it, though. "Apolla hired us to test you. We had orders not to seriously harm you, so this wasn't a true threat. She said you might be worth working with, and wanted to see if that was true. If you weren't capable of handling a two-person attack on your own turf, she wouldn't waste time on you."

"What if we'd killed you?" Trey asked.

Jack shrugged. His gesture was awkward due to his hands being behind his back. "Then we didn't deserve the job she'd hired us for and it would be our problem. Meanwhile, she'd be rid of contractors who couldn't get the job done."

A small frown appeared between Trey's eyebrows. Reece didn't know what life was like where he was from, but there people must make things like this much more complicated. As far as she was concerned, Apolla's methods were direct and pragmatic. Reece didn't even mind that Apolla had given them a little bit of a test.

In fact, it meant that Apolla had an interest in serving them well, because she believed an association with Reece and Trey would be beneficial.

Suddenly, the night reversed itself. Instead of being a crap sandwich of a bad time, it now presented a tantalizing opportunity.

Potentially.

"So now that you've done your bit, what's next?" Reece asked.

Jack shrugged again. "Up to you. You can march me over to her and demand an explanation if you want. You can release me and have me take a message to her. Whatever."

She started to like Jack, just a little. He had professionalism. He didn't get all belligerent and obnoxious because he'd failed to best them. He was just here to do a job.

So was she.

"Let's all go see her. I assume we can release your

arms and you'll act like a civilized person?"

"If I were going to try something, I'd hardly tell you so, but yeah." Jack nodded.

Trey released him but remained tense; ready to react if necessary. "Let's go, then. Hopefully Apolla is expecting us to show up at her place unannounced."

ARRANGEMENTS
DATE: 05.26.8948 (Adjusted Gregorian)
LOCATION: Apolla's Apartment, Ohiyo, Akonwara
REGION: Machete System, PED 4B, Orion Freedom Alliance

"I'm pleased. This all played out better than I'd hoped. And fast, too. I like that." Apolla sat perched on the edge of one of her uncomfortable chairs.

"So what's your game now?" Trey asked.

"No game." Apolla gave her head a quick shake that made her pale blond hair swing behind her. "Just business. I've tracked down the location of your guy Erving, as well as the identities of the two who grabbed him. I'm going to give you that information free and clear."

"What's the catch?" Reece asked. She didn't want to receive favors she'd have to pay back later. She preferred to pay in cash.

"None. Consider this my business card. A little demonstration of how I can help you. Now you know, and will bring business my way in the future, one way or another. And if I come to you looking for something, you can be assured that if I promise you a future favor, it will be well worth your effort." Apolla smiled smugly, like a cat who knew that the mouse had been cornered.

Reece liked Apolla's confidence and her knowledge of her own value. She looked at Jack. "You don't need to be here for the next part, but good luck to your future endeavors."

Jack backed toward the door. "You too. Thanks for

not taking it personally."

Reece shrugged. "Comes with the job."

Jack smiled for the first time. "So it does. See you out there."

After the door had closed behind him, Reece fixed her full attention on Apolla. "So where is Erving, who took him, and why?"

Apolla shook her head. "Figuring out why is your job, not mine. But he's only ten kilometers away, in midtown. He's being held in an apartment, so his condition might not be too bad. But the surveillance footage showed that he didn't go willingly, so who knows for sure. He went into the apartment and has not left it. Two men and a woman have come and gone at regular intervals, no doubt assigned to keep watch over him."

"So who are they?" Trey had once again chosen to lean against the wall rather than sit on the unpleasant furniture.

Apolla let out a small breath. "That appears to be somewhat complicated and out of my scope. I can give you their identities and their location, but figuring the rest out is, again, your job and not mine. All I can tell you for sure is that they do work for Pritney-Dax, but as contractors, not exclusive employees."

Reece frowned. "So they could be working for basically anyone."

Apolla nodded. "Bad news, that. They'll be reluctant to reveal their employer. You'll either need to apply sufficient force, or offer them something valuable enough to make it worth betraying their employer."

"Any particular advice on what they'd find valuable?" Trey asked. "Outside of just money, I mean."

Apolla pressed her thumb to her lips thoughtfully. "Money and opportunity are the two options. I don't know what you might be able to offer them in the way of opportunity. Contractors are always looking for a salaried position, but I don't think you're in a position to offer them that."

"Not at the moment," Reece muttered. "Anyway, thanks. We'll be in touch."

"I hope so." Apolla's smile made it clear that in spite of her cautious words, she was sure she'd be hearing from them.

After reviewing the address and reviewing the guard schedule that Apolla had sent via the Link, Reece and Trey decided to sit in the stairwell and do a little research before going over.

While Reece was searching for information on the two men who had initially grabbed Erving, Trey blinked and focused on her.

She expected him to make a joke, but he didn't.

"I don't like this hiding stuff," he said. "Staying off the grid, as you call it. It's not a good feeling."

She paused her research, knowing he wouldn't mention it if it wasn't really bothering him. "I don't either. Not only is it wildly inconvenient, but it also makes me feel like a criminal or second-class citizen. I had enough of that when I was a kid."

He nodded slowly. "Yeah, that's the feeling. We haven't done anything we weren't supposed to do as part of our job. Why are we suddenly the ones in hiding?

It has me wondering if I made the wrong choice in landing here."

He'd worked his way through a number of star systems, looking for a place to settle down and call home. Was he thinking of moving on?

With surprise, Reece realized how much she disliked that idea. She'd only just gotten accustomed to the push and pull of having someone relying on her, but also having someone she could rely on. "It's just a bad turn of events," she assured him. "But we'll figure it out and set things right."

"You sure?"

There was no way for her to know that for certain, but he needed reassurance, so she said, decisively, "Yes. Of course."

She couldn't tell if he believed her or not, but he nodded. Maybe it was enough that she said it, even if it weren't entirely certain.

His eyes lost focus, indicating he'd gone back to digging up what he could find on Carvel and Paul, the two contractors who had abducted Erving.

Poor Erving. Reece had barely spared his experience and feelings any thought. She didn't know how he'd handle something like this. Though kidnapping could happen to anyone, it wasn't a common occurrence for assistants.

Carvel and Paul looked to her like any low-level pair of people willing to do dirty work for others. They'd only become contractors to Pritney-Dax four months ago, which must have been a boon to them, but not enough to keep them from also picking up a security gig here or a creditor shakedown there. It was all smalltime stuff, though. Nothing linked them to anyone significant.

So smalltime contractors had gotten pulled in to keep a corporate executive assistant under wraps.

Why?

There was only one way to find out.

Reece waited until Trey's eyes refocused on her and nodded.

"Let's go," he said.

She was ready.

* * * * *

They took a taxi to a back alley that led to the apartment. Reece hoped Erving was in good shape. She'd always thought of him as a sensitive, thoughtful kind of guy, and doubted he'd do well under abusive conditions.

The back entrance didn't have cameras, but it did have a sturdy lock. However, it was an old, uncomplicated lock that Trey was able to simply break apart.

As much as she disliked augments on principle, they really did come in handy sometimes.

They slid inside the building and hurried up the stairwell.

<This building's old,> Trey said. <Door mechanisms are sturdy, but simple. I should be able to pop the door myself.>

<By all means,> she answered, <have at it.>

Reece was in full assault mode when they got to the third floor, made two turns, and Trey smashed the door right in.

It felt pretty good to burst right in, Righty and Lefty in her hands, and demand, "Everyone on the ground!"

Yeah, pretty good indeed. Much better than all that waiting around stuff.

A man—the guard named Paul, though Reece wasn't certain—lay on the floor. It appeared he'd dropped to his knees, then simply put his chest to the ground, because he'd stuck his ass straight up in the air. It was an odd choice, but sometimes people performed poorly under pressure.

Reece nodded to Trey and he stood guard over the man. She pushed further into the apartment, ready for someone to jump out at any second. But they didn't.

She pushed open the door to the only bedroom.

Erving blinked up at her from a rocking chair. "Oh, hello. I was wondering when you'd get here."

* * * * *

"So you expected me to come?" Reece asked.

They'd secured the guard and Trey watched the entry in case someone else arrived. Meanwhile, Reece talked to Erving within earshot of Trey. Not a difficult thing to ensure, since the apartment was economy-sized.

"Of course. You expected me to meet you, and suspicious events had already begun to unfold. I figured it would only be a matter of time until you found me." Erving seemed fine. Calm. Unharmed.

His confidence in her might be a little bit too high, but since that might benefit her in the future, she chose not to address it.

Reece said, "What information can you give me? Most important things first."

Erving paused for a moment, then said, "I believe I was taken as leverage against Schramm. I'm not sure why. My captors know he's missing, but don't seem to know his location. I think it means that either they're not working for whoever took Schramm, or Schramm disappeared on his own."

"Do you have any idea why he'd do that?" she asked.

"I have a couple of theories."

Those theories would wait until later. Reece had to deal with the immediate situation first. Plus, she didn't want the person they'd captured listening to that conversation.

"What about that guy?" She jerked a thumb over her shoulder, in the man's direction.

"I've been treated well, other than being forced to stay here and not have any outside contact." He pointed to a collar-style necklace he wore. "This blocks me from using the Link. They slapped it on me immediately."

She nodded. "I figured they had you blocked. Otherwise, I'd have heard from you. Unless you were in on it all, of course."

Erving's eyes widened and he started to speak, but Reece cut him off.

"It was an outside possibility. I didn't think it was true."

Erving closed his mouth and nodded, mollified.

Reece continued, "Any idea who wanted you locked down? Who the three captors are working for?"

"The name Boyce slipped out of them twice. It's an unusual name, so I believe it refers to a mid-level exec at Pitney-Dax."

That lined up with the information Apolla had given Reece and Trey.

"What do you know about this Boyce?" she asked. "Does he have a reason to want you out of the picture? Or to have a grudge against Schramm?"

"On the contrary. Boyce Greenley has worked closely with Schramm in the past. They went to school together."

Reece frowned. She hadn't expected that answer. "Could they be friends? I mean, as much as execs can be friends with other execs."

Erving nodded. "I believe they're at least on friendly terms."

That put a new spin on things. She had a passing familiarity with Boyce Greenley, and given what she knew of him, she could imagine a friendly relationship between him and Schramm.

"Are we going to leave this place?" Erving asked. "I'm sure my mother is very worried."

"Not yet," Reece said. "We've walked into the middle of something, and I don't want to mix things up until I have a better picture of things."

"What, then?"

"I'm going to contact Boyce Greenley and invite him over here for a chat. He may be the connection we need to make things start falling into place."

* * * * *

Two hours later, Boyce arrived. The woman who had been guarding Erving had also arrived for her shift. That meant that the small apartment was now crammed with six people, which was a bit much for the tight space.

Trey stood with his back to the door, which Reece thought was a good space saver, while also ensuring that no one tried to make a break for it—it was also necessary to keep the door in place as he'd broken the upper hinge when he'd kicked it in.

She, Erving, and Boyce sat compliantly, leaving the two low-level employees to sit on the floor, looking uneasy.

Reece didn't blame them for looking uncomfortable. They'd failed in one of their primary duties—not getting caught. Depending on how Boyce viewed the situation, this could end very badly for them.

"I'll get straight to the point," Reece said. "Because frankly, I'm tired of being in the dark and tired of waiting around. It appears that we all know that Schramm Matthews has gone missing. Meanwhile, you've imprisoned Schramm's assistant. And yet Erving here believes you're not responsible for Schramm's disappearance. I, however, am not so sure."

Boyce nodded to her. "I understand your distrust. If I were in your place, I'd feel the same way. But if you look at the facts, you'll see that it makes no sense for me to have had Schramm abducted. There's no way for me to benefit from it, since we work for rival corporations. Unless you think I'd go for a tawdry kidnap-for-ransom scenario, which would be breathtakingly stupid, considering my career track. I'll be an upper level management within three years. Why would I risk that when the golden apple is within my reach?"

Reece shook her head. "I don't know."

"I wouldn't. Like I said, there's nothing to gain, long term, and much to lose."

Trey spoke up, arms crossed over his chest looking terribly imposing. "So why kidnap Erving here? Were you hoping to blackmail Schramm with him? There are few worse things to do to an exec than making a personal assistant disappear."

"Not a bad theory," Boyce said. "But Schramm and I are on good terms. He and I can negotiate, and that makes us allies, not rivals. I would never kill that relationship by committing such an act."

"Then what?" Trey asked.

"I'm protecting Erving. Surprised?" Boyce's mouth turned up into a small smile.

Trey and Reece exchanged a look. As odd at it seemed for Boyce to protect Erving, it had a certain ring of truth.

"Why?" Reece asked.

"Because just as you had homed in on him, so had others. From my company and the other three. Nothing good was going to happen." Boyce's expression turned grim.

"Why not just tell me that, then?" Erving demanded, looking annoyed.

Boyce looked at him. "If I had said, 'You're in danger, come with me if you want to live, because I can provide you with a place to hide and people to guard you' would you have believed me? Or would you have assumed I was planning to make you disappear?"

Erving admitted, "I'd have thought you had a bullseye on my face." He straightened. "You mean these people were looking out for me and keeping me away from the people you mentioned?"

"Yep. They were under orders to get you secured, by any means necessary. And to keep you secured, because I suspected that if you found out—even after the fact—that you weren't actually a captive, you'd insist on contacting people or doing something that would expose you."

Erving's guilty expression confirmed Boyce's suspicion.

Trey rubbed his forehead. "This is getting convoluted. Okay. So you know Schramm is missing. You have some suspicions as to why. You protected Erving, through devious but effective means. So, who has Schramm?"

Boyce hesitated. "I'm not certain of this, but I suspect no one does. I think he's gone into hiding on his own."

That didn't sound right. "Why would he go into hiding without telling me?" Reece demanded.

"Two possibilities," Boyce said. "Either he's protecting you, or he wants you to come looking for him."

Reece rubbed her face with her hands. Trey was right. This *was* getting convoluted, all this chess-game gambit stuff. Move and countermove. Why did it have to be so complicated? She much preferred a good point-and-shoot scenario.

She needed to distill all of this into a plan of action. "Okay. So, if he wants me to find him, it should be fairly easy, because he'd have left clues. And if he's trying to protect me, he'd have done the exact opposite. Either way, we need to start looking for him. So where do we start?"

* * * * *

Boyce hadn't stayed long enough for their meeting, in Reece's opinion. However, for him, it was the beginning of the workday and he had to continue as if nothing were amiss.

Erving had agreed to remain, and to avoid contacting anyone. Meanwhile, Reece and Trey had some time to process the situation and change tactics.

She wished she could visit the Ringtoad. Reece did some of her best thinking bellied up to the bar with a whiskey in her hand. Such a public venue involved more risk than she wanted to take, though. They needed to stay out of sight—not to mention painting a target on Kippy's head was not the sort of thing that friends—or whatever they were now—did to one another.

That left her back at the safehouse, getting her head around the situation.

First question: Did Schramm want her to find him, or was he protecting her?

If he had intentionally left a trail for her to follow, she hadn't found it yet. Not by accident and not by searching for the rest of that day. Nothing stood out to her. No clues, no possibilities to follow up on.

It seemed unlikely he'd make it so hard if he wanted her to figure it out.

Second question: Assuming he was trying to protect her by concealing his whereabouts, how would he go about that?

He'd go somewhere she wouldn't think of. Somewhere that couldn't be easily researched.

Where?

That was the question that stumped her. Schramm was too smart to use his accounts, so she couldn't trace that. He'd have told no one but Erving about a retreat or hideaway, and Erving sure didn't know of one.

Schramm would have to get money from somewhere, though. Travel, food, and other essentials were unavoidable. He'd have to pay for them somehow.

One of Reece's more powerful methods of working as a fixer was tracking where money went, or where it came from. It almost always provided illuminating answers.

Okay, then. How to find the hidden money source of a hidden person, when she had no associated transactions?

Reece needed more.

She didn't have more.

"Ugh."

Lying down on the bed, she put her hands over her eyes. There was no trail. Nothing to follow.

Wait. Reece sat upright. If she couldn't find Schramm, then she had to make him want to reach out to her.

But how?

An idea formed in her brain and she laughed. Yep. That'd do it. Schramm would be sure to notice it, too—wherever he was.

It would work. She was sure of it.

* * * * *

"Are you sure, honey? It seems like the last kind of attention you want to have. Once I sound the alarm, there's no taking it back." Aunt Ruth sounded anxious over the audible call connection.

"I'm sure," Reece promised. "If you report me as a missing person, that will put some things into motion that I need to happen."

Schramm would surely notice, and realize she'd gotten caught up in what was happening with him. He'd reach out.

"Plus," Reece added, "it lends credence to the idea that you don't know where I am."

"I *don't* know where you are," Aunt Ruth pointed out.

"Which is also good."

"Okay. If you're sure, I'll do it right away."

"Good." Reece wished she didn't have to worry her aunt. "I'm sorry about all this. Are you doing okay?"

"Fine. We're all just fine. Dex and Rio miss you, but Kippy and I are keeping them busy."

"Wait, do you have Dex at your house?" Reece asked.

"Yes, the poor thing gets too anxious when he's left alone for long, so I had Kippy bring him over. And Kippy visits frequently."

"That's good. I hope I'll be able to come home soon. I have to get some things worked out first, though." Reece didn't want to underscore just how serious the situation was, but her aunt wasn't dumb. Aunt Ruth would know the situation had to be significant if Reece wanted to be reported as missing.

"Just do what you need to do, sweetie. I'll be here when you get home just like always."

"Thanks, Aunt Ruth. You're the best."

"I sure am. Love you, kiddo."

Reece smiled. "Love you, too."

The connection closed, and Reece felt unexpectedly melancholy.

At least things had been put into motion. Schramm would reach out once he saw she was listed as missing.

Unless he was dead. Or somehow involved in something.

No, he'd reach out.

He had to.

INCOMMUNICADO

DATE: 05.27.8948 (Adjusted Gregorian)
LOCATION: Tommy's Safehouse, Near Ohiyo, Akonwara
REGION: Machete System, PED 4B, Orion Freedom Alliance

For a full day, Reece had been officially missing—and she hadn't heard from Schramm.

If he was alive, and able to check the Link, he'd have found out about it almost immediately. He had customized alerts for notices about people who had close contact with him. There was no way he'd miss it.

A terrible feeling started to grow inside her as she roamed around the safehouse. What if Schramm were dead? Or comatose? Or simply imprisoned and cut off from Link access?

She'd never find him.

Further, if he was dead, and Rexcare was also after Reece, it didn't bode well.

A knock at her room door—which she'd left ajar—snapped her out of her reverie.

"Come in."

Trey edged in cautiously. "You've been quiet."

"I've been trying to think us out of this. I haven't been very successful. I'm starting to believe we've got no avenues left to follow."

Trey sat on the edge of her bed, and his weight made it shift beneath Reece. "I'm reluctant to suggest it, but I think it may be time to get out of Machete," he said soberly. "Go someplace where just going out in public won't be a risk. We really don't have a fighting chance here, long term."

Reece sighed. "I'm reluctant to admit it, but I just came to that conclusion myself. We could get out of the system, wait for things to cool off. Come back when some answers have surfaced."

Assuming answers ever *did* surface. They might not, and she didn't say it out loud, because they were both already all too aware.

She nodded. "Okay. Let's get ready to leave Machete—or at least Akonwara—indefinitely. If we haven't heard from Schramm by the time we're ready, we'll go."

Four hours later, they'd done their packing and converted the anonymous account she'd been using, for outsystem access. The packing itself had taken little time. They'd arrived at the safehouse with nothing but what they'd been wearing, and had bought little in the time since. At least Reece wouldn't have a lot of luggage to carry.

There could be no goodbyes. She'd let Aunt Ruth and Kippy know she'd left after she'd gotten some good distance away. Reece had to think about their safety, since they'd still be on Akon.

It sucked a really, really excessive amount, but sometimes that was just what life gave her.

"Autotaxi's here," Trey said.

"Right." Reece lifted her bag and suppressed a sigh. There was no point in expressing her unhappiness. Instead—with forced false enthusiasm— she said, "Off on another adventure."

Trey didn't look convinced, but at least she'd made

the effort.

They loaded the autotaxi with their things and headed for the transit station that would take them to the spaceport and then away from Akon.

* * * * *

"It's going to be forty minutes before our shuttle boards." Trey frowned at the delay, but there was nothing they could do but wait.

The spaceport was busy that day, with lots of traders arriving and departing.

"I'm going to go get a smoothie," Reece decided. She hadn't eaten much that day, and her stomach was gurgling. A smoothie would be easy to consume, even with the ugly feelings rolling through her gut. "Want something?"

"Sure, I'll have whatever you get." Trey smiled, but Reece could tell he was forcing it. He didn't want to leave Akon either.

They both wanted to stay and fight. It was in their nature. But even so, staying to fight in the face of inevitable failure was stupid if they could flee and return to fight another day.

"I'll get you the extra-extra-large size," she said.

Trey gave her a thumbs-up, and they both pretended to be amused.

Neither of them was fooled, but pretending was all they had left.

Reece bought berry-flavored smoothies for them— hers a mere medium while Trey's portion easily tripled hers.

She let out a sigh when he took the cup from her, rolling her shoulder as if he'd just relieved her of a great burden.

He smirked at her.

They sat quietly, letting time pass as they drank their smoothies. There was little to say. They'd agreed to take the first flight out of the Machete system, and it didn't really matter where it took them. They'd deal with whatever came next when it happened.

"You packed your nutrition supplements, right?" Trey asked. "You never know what the food will be like wherever we end up."

"Hah." She recognized his deadpan humor when she heard it. "Of course, I did. But I bet you've seen a big range of cuisine in all the places you've been."

"Oh, yeah. Pretty much everything you can think of."

"What was the best?"

He thought for a long moment. "It's hard to say, because there have been a lot of great dishes, but they're good in different ways. I can say that the mushroom ramen we had the other day measures up with the best of them."

"Okay, how about the worst?" she asked.

"Live squid heads. I just couldn't. I tried really hard, because it was a welcome meal, and not eating them was an insult, but, damn, no way. Nuh uh." He shook his head emphatically.

Reece smiled. "Sounds pretty gross."

"I don't want to judge other people's ways...but yeah. I mean, the squids were *looking* at me with their eye stalks." He set his cup aside to demonstrate, using his fingers as eyestalks and pointing them at her. He shuddered.

An old woman in a faded yellow dress passed them, walking with a slight limp. She stood out from other travelers, but Reece had seen hundreds of women like her growing up in Slagside. Thousands, even.

Women who had aged badly thanks to hard labor and time spent under the twin stars' light. In spite of the limp, the woman had broad shoulders and bigger arms than most. Her stringy hair looked like it hadn't been washed in months. No doubt, the water to do so cost too much for her.

There were some things about Akon that Reece didn't mind leaving behind.

She mentally wished the woman well. Maybe she was headed somewhere that would be better for her. Maybe she'd won an interstellar ticket to somewhere she could make a new start.

As if she'd heard Reece, the woman paused and turned just as she passed.

"Could you show an old lady to the loo?" she asked.

Wait. That wasn't a woman's voice.

Reece peered at the face and stared in shock at Schramm Matthews. For a moment, she couldn't speak. Even when she could, she wasn't sure what to lead with.

"You can't leave," he hissed. "They'll get you up there before you get through the gate."

"What do we do, then?" she asked.

Schramm returned to his old lady voice, "Help me out to the autotaxi, dear. My legs aren't what they used to be."

Reece rose and took his arm, handing her smoothie cup to Trey. Helping an old lady wouldn't look suspicious.

Trey disposed of the cups, then trailed them. Watching, no doubt, for anyone paying them any particular interest or coming too close.

"Car's over here," Schramm muttered, hitching his elbow forward and to the side. "The blue one. Just pretend you two are picking up Granny and taking her home."

Reece thought of their bags, which were still inside. Oh well. There hadn't been much in there anyway.

She helped 'Granny' into the car, then ran around to the other side, only to find Trey already getting in. She got in the front seat instead.

As soon as Schramm entered a destination and they took off, Reece burst out with the first of the many questions that had occurred to her.

"What's going on?"

Schramm pulled his wig off and dropped it to the floor. He let out a long sigh. "Bad stuff. I thought I'd protected you from it, but apparently not."

"So you *were* protecting us." For some reason, that knowledge made Reece feel better. "But why did you make it impossible to find you?"

"Because being with me is not good for you. I thought if I distanced myself from you and had no contact, they'd leave you and Erving alone. They'd assume I didn't trust you and you weren't loyal to me, and they wouldn't bother with you. Apparently, I was wrong."

"Erving got grabbed soon after you disappeared."

Schramm cringed. "Any clue where he is?"

"Yeah. He's safe and under guard, thanks to your pal Boyce."

Schramm sat up straighter, wearing a look of hopeful surprise. "Really?"

"Yeah, he's in your corner. Loyal. His first concern after making sure you were okay was taking care of your people."

"Wow." Schramm seemed to be having trouble processing that.

"Is it so surprising?" Trey asked. "He said you went to school together."

"Yeah, we did. It's just…" Schramm shrugged. "This is Akon, and we're both in the hierarchy of big five companies. There's been no one I could *really* trust in a very long time."

"What about me?" Reece asked, insulted.

"Not even you. You don't know a person's loyalty until it's tested, as the saying goes."

Trey looked at Reece and she smiled. He said, "Yeah, she was telling me the same thing not long ago. At least you two are on the same page."

"Okay." Schramm looked suddenly enlivened. Energized. "We've got us three, Erving, and Boyce. That's not too bad." His expression turned calculating.

"And Apolla," Reece added. "She's a one-woman surveillance company, along with some contractors she uses, and she's pretty deep in the game."

"Game?" Schramm asked.

"I mean she's got connections. And she knows how to

get things done. She sent over a couple guys to see if we were competent."

"And...?" Schramm seemed a little afraid of the answer.

"I shot the hand off one of them." Reece grinned. She held her hand in the shape of a gun and said, "Pew."

Trey laughed. "Pew? It was more like a bang, followed by a huge clap."

Reece laughed too. It wasn't that funny, but about a minute ago, they'd been fleeing the system in fear and now things were looking so very much better.

Trey was smiling, a combative gleam in his eye. He hadn't liked the idea of running away, either.

When Reece looked at Schramm, he had the same gleam, and she felt her spirits lift.

Oh, yeah. It was their turn to start making shit happen.

Finally.

BACKEND OF NOWHERE

DATE: 05.28.8948 (Adjusted Gregorian)
LOCATION: Schramm's Farm, Agriculture Sector 43, Akonwara
REGION: Machete System, PED 4B, Orion Freedom Alliance

Reece, Trey, and Schramm spent the rest of that day traveling to Schramm's remote hideout, deep within an agricultural district.

The autotaxi—which had turned out to be Schramm's personal property and actually could be driven by a person as well—turned down a long gravel lane and they bumped along for a good twenty minutes before arriving at an old farmhouse.

Other than looking dusty—common during the hot season—the building appeared to be in good repair, its wraparound porch even featured a hanging swing-bench that looked particularly inviting. Window boxes—though empty of flowers—still added a homey touch.

"This is nice. Whose is it?" Trey asked.

"Mine. Technically, it belongs to a guy named Nyonga, but since he doesn't actually exist, it's mine."

"Why keep it off your records?" Reece asked. "Tax evasion?"

Schramm chuckles. "Hardly. I have to pay more to keep it in a fictitious name. I made all this mine, so I can get off the grid every now and then. I rarely manage it, but sometimes I get a weekend to myself and I come out here. This place is my motivation to make it to retirement age and have a chance to slow down and count the seconds of the days."

Reece had always wondered if the corporate grind ever got to him. Apparently, it did.

In spite of having worked for him for years, she knew very little about Schramm outside the workplace. There was a reason, of course—he pretty much embodied his job and devoted himself to it entirely. As a result, Reece knew almost nothing about the man himself. Likewise, he knew little about her on a personal level.

She imagined that living in close quarters with him would change all that. It should prove interesting.

Instructive, even.

"What about you two?" Schramm asked as they entered the farmhouse. "Have you ever thought about what your reward for all this would be?"

Reece and Trey looked at each other and shrugged.

"Survival?" Trey suggested. "I kind of get the feeling you come from a background that Reece and I can't really relate to. And even between us, there are huge differences."

Reece slid a finger across a decorative mantel that served as the focal point of a large living room. She wasn't surprised to find a layer of dust. "I come from Slagside. We don't have a concept of retirement, really. I mean, I do now, but where I grew up, you expected to be on the hustle your whole life. The only reward was not dying."

Schramm didn't look taken aback, or even surprised. "I know very well where you both came from. But that doesn't represent your current status in life. You've managed to climb higher than your childhood peers.

That makes me curious. So what is it you hope the future brings you?"

Reece found the line of questioning odd. Was Schramm as curious about them as they were about him? "I want what anyone wants. Security. Ideally, some kind of happiness would be built into that."

Trey nodded. "I want a place where I can exist peacefully. Carve out a living. Have some good times here and there."

Schramm whistled. It was the first time Reece had ever heard him do so.

"You two don't aim for much, do you?" Schramm turned his back on them and strolled away.

Reece and Trey looked at each other. Were they supposed to follow?

Shrugging, they followed. It wasn't like they had anything to unpack, so why not?

Schramm moseyed through a dining room, a kitchen, and out the back door.

Apparently, the porch wrapped all the way around the house. Reece stepped out and found the heat mitigated a great deal by the shade and heat shielding of the porch's cover.

"Wow." Reece gazed out at what she suspected was hundreds of acres of property. A pergola led through a flower garden that had little color at the moment, but which must be gorgeous during a non-perihelion year. A vegetable garden sprawled east to west past the flowers, and beyond that, an orchard. She couldn't identify the types of trees, but she suspected they were both fruit and nut varieties.

Reece took a long, deep breath. "Ahh. It smells good here."

Trey walked out toward the gardens. "Anything growing this time of year?"

Schramm joined him. "A few things. Some of our horticulture actually thrives during the hot season and has developed a lifecycle that centers on the perihelion. Isn't that interesting?"

Reece spotted another porch swing and decided that a house with a full wraparound porch, two porch swings, and an orchard, earned her full approval.

She promptly sat on the swing, letting the men go look at plants. She'd enjoy the shade and the swing, and wish she had some tea or lemonade to sip.

Being on the run for their lives notwithstanding, this was kind of a sweet setup.

And who would have thought Schramm enjoyed gardening? Surely he had someone to take care of things when he couldn't be around—which was most of the time—but there he was, bending over a pepper plant with Trey and talking about rhizomes and stuff.

Reece was getting to know him better already.

Stretching out, she put her hands behind her head and closed her eyes. She let out a deep breath. Aunt Ruth would love it here. Dex would adore all the trees, which were hard to come by in the vicinity of the commercial district. And Kippy would set up a bounceball net or something, and somehow manage to bring dozens of people there for endless games and fun.

Maybe she should think about making a place like this her retirement goal, too. It wasn't like she could be chasing people down in her golden years. She had probably twenty more years ahead of her in this position, tops. If she hadn't saved enough to support herself and Aunt Ruth, she'd be in trouble, because she wasn't likely to find another decent job after that.

Reece possessed a very specific skillset, after all. One which didn't translate well to other industries. Though she had great business sense, she'd probably respond incredibly poorly to a customer who insisted on being unreasonable. One simply couldn't kill customers and stay in business. It was one or the other, and she knew which she'd end up choosing, sooner or later.

Likewise with customer service positions. Reece simply wasn't equipped for that kind of work.

Of course, she was getting ahead of herself. At the moment, she had no actual employment since, for whatever reason, Rexcare had turned against Schramm, and subsequently Reece, due to her association with him.

She sat up. All right. Time to make some lemonade. She went back inside to the kitchen and began rummaging through cabinets for lemons and sugar.

She'd squeeze the hell out of everything about the situation she was in and come up with something good, even if it killed her.

* * * * *

After making a tall pitcher of lemonade in the most brutal of hands-on methods, Reece felt refreshed and ready to take the fight to Rexcare.

"It's time to talk real dirt," she said as Schramm

poured each of them a glass of lemonade on the back porch.

Schramm set the pitcher down. "Do you want to hear what I know, or what I suspect?"

"Let's start with what you know," Trey said.

Schramm ran his fingers absently over a cloth napkin, gathering his thoughts. "I've had the sense that something was off for a few months. I'm always busy, but the amount of work shoved on me was extreme. Not only that, but it wasn't entirely necessary. Underlings could have done a good bit of it, but it somehow kept coming my way. So, I started thinking, what would be the purpose of keeping me so busy?"

"Distracting you," Reece answered.

Schramm nodded. "That's what I thought. So, I started paying closer attention to what others at the top end of Rexcare have been doing. Pretty soon, I noticed a pattern. All of the extra work was coming from Cooper Fields. Indirectly, for the most part, but at his behest all the same."

Trey tapped his fingers on the small tray they were using as a table, which made the glasses all jiggle ever so slightly. "So you had your 'who'. Then you needed the 'what.'"

"Right. And that was made easier by the fact that the 'why' was pretty obvious. Why else would Cooper busy me? Whether it was to try to make me look bad, to make my life hard, or to distract me, it all pointed at him making a play for my job."

"Why?" Reece asked. "He already has a top-level position on par with yours."

"Eh, the title is on par, but I've been with the company longer and that seniority gives me an edge over him. Plus, more of the board members are on my side. Since I have no intentions of retiring for another decade or two, the only way to get to the top is to get rid of me." Schramm didn't look angry—merely matter-of-fact.

"That doesn't make you mad?" Reece asked. "I'd feed him his feet for breakfast."

Schramm smiled. "It annoys me, but it's not an uncommon approach. Besides, that's why people like me employ people like you, so our enemies end up eating their feet anyway."

Trey frowned at Reece. "You don't actually do that, do you?"

"Nah. Too messy. But I'm not above letting them suffer in other ways if they've inspired some spite in me."

"So I guess the guy with the hand didn't get that treatment. The way we packed him off to the hospital was downright neighborly of us." Trey looked thoughtful.

She shrugged. "I didn't get the feeling they were a real threat, and it turned out they weren't. It worked out."

"Except for the hand guy. Cliff."

"I'm sure he received an injury bonus from Apolla and got his medical expenses paid." Reece noticed that Schramm merely sipped his lemonade, refraining from asking questions about Cliff-the-hand-guy and whatever had transpired between them.

"Anyway," she said, "back to the story."

"There's not a lot more to it," Schramm said. "Thanks to my diligence, I realized that Cooper had been working on framing me for an embezzling scheme. Since my life in Machete would be over after such a thing, he also kindly arranged for me to commit suicide. All things considered, I thought it best to get myself out of his reach. Plus, going off the grid kept him from being able to enact the final parts of the embezzling frame-up, because I wouldn't have been around to do the things he intended to say I'd done."

"So your reputation hasn't been ruined," Trey mused. "That's good."

Schramm ran a finger down the side of his glass, catching a bead of condensation. "Well, my reputation has certainly taken a hit for disappearing. No doubt Cooper could have made the embezzling thing work with my disappearance if he'd had just a little more time. But it doesn't look good for me all the same. A person who's done no wrong doesn't just disappear from a job like mine without a word."

"At least it's repairable," Reece said. "We can get the proof, thwart Cooper, and return you alive and well to Rexcare. And us, too." She pointed to Trey and herself.

"And Erving," Trey added.

"Oh, yeah. Poor Erving. I almost forgot about him." Reece felt a tinge of guilt.

"The good news is that I've planned ahead for this kind of corporate espionage, and there are Link backups that will prove Cooper's responsibility for all of his machinations."

Trey squinted at Schramm. "I'm going to guess there's a big heaping helping of bad news to make that bit of good news not look nearly so good. Otherwise, you'd have already grabbed those backups and nailed his ass to the wall."

"Right." Schramm looked pained. "The problem is that Cooper has used his personal connections to make sure I can't get access to a lot of the places that might be helpful to me. One of those places is in a Rexcare datacenter, and that's where the files we need are. There's no getting them remotely. It's an in-only pathway, to keep the node from being tampered with or stolen from."

Reece set her glass of lemonade, nearly empty now, on the table. "So we need to break into this place and get the proof. How's their security?"

"Strong," Schramm said.

Reece grinned and cracked her knuckles. "Sounds like this is going to be fun, then."

* * * * *

Reece surveyed her team, feeling like this was a special moment in her life. She wasn't likely to get many opportunities to lead a frontal assault like this, and she planned to make the most of it.

She'd put a lot of effort into the attack, after all. It had taken negotiations, promises, and a few assurances of future personal favors to put all this together. Plus, they'd had to reach out to some people that they'd been staying away from, in order to protect them.

But they needed every person they could trust in on this one.

Trey, Schramm, and Reece were all in, of course. But they needed someone who could hack into a data storage system in a short amount of time, and none of them had those skills.

Reece turned around to smile at Marky, who rode in the taxivan behind her. Marky, thrilled to be along on something with such high stakes, smiled back.

Before she'd opened her betting lounge, Marky had made her money with some ingenious hacking skills. Once she'd saved the capital, she'd gotten out of that highly dangerous business and started Debtor's Haven. She hadn't even dabbled in hacking ever since—until now.

Beside Marky, Apolla stared out the dark-tinted window. She wore an intense expression. Schramm had offered her a very large amount of money, but payout was contingent on the operation's success.

In the third row of seats, Trey occupied the center with Raya on his left, looking serious but determined. Reece hadn't been sure about soliciting her help. She didn't think Raya cared enough—not about Schramm or Reece herself—to go this far out for them. Also, Raya's position at Donnercorp was too good to lose on something that wasn't a direct benefit to her. But Trey had insisted, and Reece had relented. It would seem that their relationship had gotten more serious than Reece had realized.

On Trey's right side, sat Tommy, eyes wide. The weapons dealer—in contrast to Apolla—seemed a little *too* enthusiastic. He appeared to vibrate with ecstatic energy. They'd have to keep a close watch on him, but there was no doubt that he'd put everything he had into the job. He'd also equipped them with an astonishing array of firepower that Reece doubted she would ever again see all loaded into one vehicle.

Yep, it was an exciting day, all right. She smiled at their driver. Kippy noticed and grinned back. He didn't have all of the details about why this was going down, but when she'd asked him if he'd drive for them, he'd immediately agreed.

Back in their youth, he'd been pretty good at retrostripping purloined autotaxis to decommission them from the fleet. He hadn't done it in quite a long time, but the principles were the same and he'd seemed to enjoy taking care of the autovan Tommy had acquired.

On Reece's other side, Schramm seemed oddly at peace with all of this highly criminal activity. She'd expected him to be nervous. Uncomfortable. Instead, he looked like he was simply going to another board meeting.

Maybe being an exec required tougher nerves than she'd previously thought.

They'd already gone over their intentions, and they all knew what part they had to play. Reece guessed that they were all thinking it over, focusing on what needed to be done, because after loading the autovan up and taking off, there'd been very little said.

A two-phase assault, followed by a by-any-means-necessary retreat required a great deal of brainpower, it seemed.

Since she had time, Reece ran over the scenario a few more times in her head, too.

Once they arrived at the security gate, Reece locked eyes with each person to make sure they were ready.

They were as ready as they'd get.

Kippy rolled to a stop at the gate, putting on an easy smile and a casual posture. "Hey, how's it going?"

He spoke to the guard as if they were old friends. Somehow, Kippy could pull that sort of thing off. If Reece had tried something like that, the person would have probably immediately slapped the emergency alarm.

But the thirtyish man smiled, blinking away some fatigue and boredom. A job like his was mostly characterized by long periods of nothing to do.

"Got your security code?" the guard asked routinely.

Kippy's smile faltered. "Uh, no. They said they'd leave it at the gate for me."

The guard's lips turned down. "Why would it make sense for them to leave the code with me, rather than give it to you? I hate when they do that stuff. It's like they're intentionally trying to cause a security breach."

"I know, right? I thought it was weird, too." Kippy rolled his eyes. "They said it was something about not being able to log in and generate a code at the time. I forget why."

The guard glanced at the van and the sign painted on the side, reading *KMA Technologies*. "You're a contractor? What's your business in there?"

"Subtransducter cables and related peripherals. We're

wiring up a room that's being converted into a new section of the datacenter. Again. You'd think they'd just build more than they need so they'd have space to expand, rather than adding them one by one. It's such a waste of money." Kippy shrugged helplessly.

"Again?" The guard shook his head. "They just finished one two months ago. I'll never understand corporate thinking."

Kippy smiled. "Same here. But at least we get paid, right?"

The guard grinned. "Yep. If they were more efficient, there'd be fewer jobs to go around. Who did you say left you a security code?"

"River." Kippy offered a name that was so common there was bound to be someone inside who went by it. Every now and then, single-name confusion could be put to good use. "I'm not sure what department, though. I forgot to ask."

The guard went back into his enclosed kiosk. Reece watched him flick through a series of displays on his sim, frowning as he went.

The guard returned. "Didn't find it. I'd give River a call, but we've got like fifteen of them, and it's almost my lunch break. Once you get to the lobby, they'll have you on the reception books and will be able to connect you to the right person and get you going to the right place."

Kippy nodded. "No problem. Don't want to make you late for lunch. It's not like they extend your time when you work the first ten minutes, right?"

"That's for sure." The guard grimaced. "Thanks, man."

"No problem." Kippy grinned, then waved when the gate opened and allowed him to proceed through.

Reece let out a breath, once again amazed at how Kippy's easy manner could smooth anything over.

First hurdle was done. It was the smallest of them, and now they had to hope the guard didn't decide to be helpful and send word up ahead that they were coming.

"Right," she said. "Now we're on. Everyone ready?"

Tommy nodded eagerly and said, "Hell yeah!" while the other responses ranged from Marky's emphatic nod and wink to Schramm's grim acceptance.

A little bit of everything.

At the main entrance of the huge complex, it was clear that money had been spent merely to impress. The architects had perpetrated a sprawling one-story design that would have been breathtakingly cost prohibitive inside the commerce district. Even out here on the outskirts, in barren land not fit for farming, it seemed shockingly wasteful. Sure, they wouldn't have to pay for elevators or spend nearly as much on quakeproofing, but the energy waste alone for a single-story complex would eclipse both of the other concerns within just a few years.

Yet Reece had to admit that the gleaming pale gray complex—laid out in a pentagon with a courtyard on the inside—had a certain stark beauty to it. Or could it truly be called a pentagon when the back side was open to provide vehicle access?

Either way, they couldn't see that end at the moment, as it was directly opposite them on the other side of the complex. Instead, the grand entrance lived up to its name, with an elegantly understated arch that soared above and created shade as one entered the building.

Schramm got out and Reece started to slide across the seat to follow him. Kippy's arm curled around her before she could move further and she turned her head to look at him.

"I guess I'm finally getting a look at what you really do." His smile was small and crooked, but there nonetheless.

"I guess so. I'll have to hope you still like me when it's all said and done," she joked.

"No worries about that." He leaned in and dropped a brief but firm kiss on her lips. "I'll see you soon."

"Good luck," she said, then addressed the rest of the team as she slid across the seat toward the door. "I know you all can do this."

She briefly made eye contact once more with Apolla, Raya, Tommy, and Marky. Her gaze lingered on Trey, who returned her look with a sharp nod.

"Go get 'em, Miss Fancypants Exec," he said.

"Pineapple?" she asked.

"Pineapple." He nodded.

She grinned as she stepped out of the car and smoothed her expensive tailored suit down. How Schramm had managed to get something so fine manufactured on such short notice, she had no idea, but she'd never felt so elegant in her life. She'd decided that charcoal gray looked damn good on her, even if she'd had to secure her hair in a businesslike knot at the back of her head.

"Ready?" Schramm asked.

"Yep. Let's go." She followed a half pace behind him,

showing deference to him as a junior executive would to a senior.

She admired how Schramm strode into the place like he owned it, or at least was a significant stakeholder — one of which may be partially true.

He stopped at the reception desk, but not as a supplicant seeking entry into the inner sanctum. Schramm's approach was something else entirely. He looked down at the receptionist, no doubt as fearsome a gatekeeper as those in the dragon's lair at Rexcare, as if the person were his messenger.

He spoke in a tone of voice only the truly privileged and important could manage. "Schramm Matthews to see Jame Bellwether."

The receptionist instantly went from dragon to mouse at the mention of the two names. Jame Bellwether was one of the top people at Trumark, which had been working to either become one of the Big Four by pushing Pritney-Dax out, or expand the Big Four to a Big Five. He'd been getting close year by year, too, with Trumark getting a stranglehold on commercial datacenters like this that serviced both corporations and the populace at large.

And of course, Schramm would be instantly recognized in a place like this, where deals were made every day to further entrench Trumark in the local economy.

"Of course, Mr. Matthews. Is Mr. Bellwether expecting you?" The man's tone was nothing like it would have been if Reece had asked to see someone.

"Not specifically. We had plans to meet sometime

soon, and I ended up in the relative vicinity and decided to take advantage of that." Schramm didn't keep his attention on the receptionist. Instead, he cast his eyes across the lobby, showing how little time he had for such a menial exchange of words.

Reece couldn't decide if she should admire such a display, or detest it, so she chose to admire his impressive show of deplorable privilege.

"Of course." Instead of ignoring Schramm, the receptionist waved over one of his co-workers. "Please show Mr. Matthews and his colleague to a hospitality suite."

The woman sprang into action, her eyes widening at the use of the "Mr." title, which was an unmistakable sign of importance, even if she didn't recognize the name itself.

"Right this way." The young woman looked like she'd barely left school, but seemed well on her way to a career in executive services. She keyed them through a door and led them briskly down a long hall before stepping aside and gesturing to the doorway, allowing them to enter before her.

Reece almost sucked in a breath at the room's opulence, but she caught herself in time. Instead, she pasted on a cool expression as she observed the plush furniture upholstered with luxury fabrics, the elaborately framed artwork on the walls, and the full array of fresh food on a sideboard, as if a buffet had been planned for them ahead of time.

"May I pour you a drink?" the young woman asked, gesturing at an open-air chiller tray that held a variety of bottles. "You must be hot from being outside."

Schramm waved her suggestion away. "We'll get it ourselves, thank you."

The young receptionist took a step back and bowed from the shoulders, having recognized Schramm's dismissive tone. "Of course. Please let us know if you need anything at all. As soon as Mr. Bellwether is available, we will let you know."

Schramm nodded and the girl hurried out, closing the door behind her.

Reece sidled up to the food. Fresh fruit, already cut, sandwiches, muffins, and pie sat on display, as if for an advertisement. "Any reason to think this stuff is poisoned or laced with trackers or something?"

Schramm shook his head. "No."

"Well good." She grabbed the plate and began piling it up with goodies. "Because I am not about to let all this go to waste."

She poured herself a sparkling water, then took it and her plate to one of the plush couches. She laughed at the idea of sitting and eating on something that probably cost the equivalent of a year's salary for her, but she did it all the same.

She sighed. "So comfy."

She took a bite of ripe purplefruit and sighed. "So delicious. We only ever have purplefruit for new year and even then, it's the frozen kind."

"Is it good?" he asked.

"Incredible."

She expected him to shrug it off, but instead, he went and put a few pieces on a plate before joining her with it and a glass of tea.

He took a bite of the juicy fruit. "You're right. This is delicious."

She wished they could communicate via the Link, but he hadn't gotten his jailbroken and they couldn't risk Rexcare listening in. He did wear a squelch collar so they couldn't track him, but otherwise, he had to refrain from using his Link. After this was done, Tommy would need to jailbreak Schramm's implants.

Unless there was a reason not to at that point.

They engaged in mundane conversation and ate while they waited. Meanwhile, if all had gone right, the others would be carrying out their assignments. They'd planned this carefully, but Reece worried she'd hear an alarm go off any minute.

So far so good, though.

A brief knock was immediately followed by the door swinging open, and a round-faced man entering. "Schramm!" the man exclaimed. "What a nice surprise."

Sure it was. This guy had been colluding against Schramm for who knew how long. Reece doubted that Bellwether had any good feelings about Schramm showing up here. But he didn't know he'd been caught, and would no doubt continue to perpetrate the charade until he knew.

"Not so nice for me," Schramm admitted. "I'm afraid I've been caught up in something not of my making. A power grab at my company."

Bellwether sat, looking concerned. "I'm sorry to hear that. How can I help?"

"I need to access some Rexcare records. We store

some of our backups here, and I think I might be able to find proof of the scheme against me there."

It was pretty close to the truth, as far as lies went.

"Of course! If you give me the location and the dates you need, I'll pull them myself. Anything for you." Bellwether gave Schramm a look of sympathy.

"I knew I could count on you. I won't forget your help." Schramm stood and offered his hand to Bellwether, who shook it.

"Never mind all that. It's the least I can do." Bellwether handed a device to Schramm, who entered some parameters that no one would ever look for.

"I'm relieved. We'll wait here, if you don't mind." Schramm looked at Reece, then said quickly, "This is my junior, by the way. She's unfortunately gotten caught up in all this due to my mentoring her."

Bellwether gave her a cursory nod, barely even glancing at her. As a junior executive, she didn't matter, and they all knew it.

As a fixer, she mattered a whole hell of a lot, and soon Bellwether couldn't fail to know it with absolute clarity.

After his smarmy behavior, she was looking forward to sticking it to him. She thought of Trey and the others, and where they were that moment. Right on plan, hopefully.

Please let them be right on plan.

She stuffed some more purplefruit in her mouth before things got crazy because it was too delicious not to, and she wanted to cost Trumark as much money as she could while she had the chance.

* * * * *

Reece was still chewing on her latest mouthful, when an alarm went off. She reached under her suit jacket to where she'd stashed her pulse pistol. A shame her Rikulfs couldn't fit in there, but they were just too big. And besides, most of the people here were innocent. Or enough so that she didn't want to actually put holes in them.

She dialed the pulse pistol all the way up and looked to Schramm. "Ready? Pretty sure we're going to have to shoot our way out of here now."

Looking grim, Schramm nodded and reached for his own pulse pistol. He'd assured her that he had decent aim, but she had reservations about him having one. The last thing any of them needed was for him to give her a blast that left her incapacitated.

Everyone always thought they'd be cool and be able to aim well in a hot situation, but the truth was, very few actually could.

On the other hand, Schramm faced down board members on a regular basis, so…she'd put even odds on him shooting her or not.

As she passed the food, she thought, what the heck, and stuffed some more fruit in her mouth.

With her cheeks puffed out, she kicked open the door and barged into the corridor. A pulse wave rippled down the corridor, too distant to do any damage, and Reece fired a trio of shots in the direction it came from.

A satisfying cry of pain came from down the wall and Reece hurried to her right, hugging the wall. This junction would bring her out to a maintenance corridor that might have less traffic.

At least, she hoped so.

A woman burst out of a door, almost banging right into her. Instinctively, Reece delivered a palm-strike to the woman's nose, which resulted in a crunch and a horrific scream.

Oops. Reece quickly gave her a pulse blast, which she should have done to begin with. The close quarters had thrown her a little. At least the woman didn't have to worry about her nose for a little bit.

"Sorry about the nose," Reece muttered as she stepped over the woman. She glanced behind her to make sure Schramm was following.

He stepped around the woman, frowning, but kept moving.

Good. He was handling the situation okay so far.

They hurried down the maintenance corridor, but the next bit would be trickier. To rendezvous with Trey and the others, they'd need to cut right through the building's lunch room.

That would hardly be inconspicuous, but the only alternative would be a circuitous route that would take them an extra ten minutes and expose them to much more potential of getting caught.

Forward, then.

Schramm grabbed her arm. "Wait!'

Reece stopped and turned to look at him. "What?"

"If we put these away, and pretend we're there to eat, we might go unnoticed."

"Seriously?" It sounded like the dumbest idea ever to

her. "Are they not broadcasting our images everywhere right now?"

"Of course not."

"What? Why not? Are they stupid?"

"No. But the alarm that went off is disguised. It *sounds* like an air purification alarm, which happens periodically and isn't a reason for alarm. But for security people and those who need to be aware, there's a tone in it that a simple air purification alarm doesn't have. They're trained to know the difference. So only certain people will even know there's a real problem right now."

"Air purification alarm." She shook her head and stared at him. "Inside an atmosphere. Where we can already breathe."

Schramm shrugged. "They're known to be finicky systems that go off frequently. It's a good cover. Plus, corporations can pretend they really care that much about their employees, and about protecting them from environmental pollutants in the workplace."

She stared at him for another long moment. "I'm a little scared that this is something you people thought of."

"What? Because it's deceptive and calculating?"

"Yeah. You all are smarter than I thought. So okay, let's stroll in there and get some biscuits. Or whatever the lunchroom is serving today."

Reece tucked her pulse pistol in her jacket pocket. Not the best carrying place, but she could get to it faster than her back holster. She opened the cafeteria door and walked in, as she imagined a hungry exec would. Calculated steps. A purposeful, yet bored expression.

For good measure, she pretended she was mentally counting all the money in her accounts. That might give her just the right amount of a 'you underlings are so far beneath me that you might actually be dirt' kind of vibe.

It *felt* pretty authentic, anyway.

She strolled up to the salad bar and paused, as if considering its options, then turned away to the counter that had the hot dishes, which was closer to the door. Then she went past it, toward the drink machines.

"Milkshakes." She stopped and looked at Schramm. "These people have milkshakes in their cafeteria. That's amazing."

He shrugged. Apparently he didn't think it was that impressive.

She grabbed a small cup and filled it. For authenticity. She slapped a lid on it and stuck a straw in.

Schramm watched her, mystified, and she gave him a pointed look. If anyone was watching, it would look awfully suspicious if they just strolled through without getting anything.

Sighing, he reached for a cup and began filling it with a chocolate-flavored shake. As soon as he'd put a straw in it, they went out the north side entrance, which connected to another maintenance corridor.

As they walked own the maintenance hall, Reece casually sipped her milkshake. For authenticity, of course. Yum, berry flavor. Her favorite.

She'd started to get pretty pleased with herself. Their escape had gone darn well so far. Outside of the woman with the broken nose.

Then a door opened and a group of three burly men

and a very pissed-off looking woman came out, pushing a floor buffer.

"If you'd done it right the first time, you wouldn't have had to—" the aggrieved woman noticed them and abruptly ended her angry tirade.

The four looked at her and Schramm.

Reece looked to him for some smooth explanation for why two execs would be in a back hall like this.

He'd gone mute.

Well, dammit.

She did the only thing she could think of. She slapped his milkshake out of his hand, causing it to splatter all over the floor and wall. "How dare you! You lure me in here saying it's a shortcut and then grab my ass? I'll report you. This isn't the Joseon era, you know. Just because I'm your junior doesn't mean you can get away with that garbage. Good luck explaining this to the shareholders!"

She stomped away indignantly, praying he had the good sense to play along and follow her, begging for forgiveness.

It took a beat too long, but he did.

When they burst out into a hallway, she started giggling. She'd remembered Trey's milkshake story, and that, combined with the horrific mess Schramm's chocolate shake had created, and the dumbfounded expressions of the floor-cleaning staff, and the accusation that Schramm had grabbed her butt…she couldn't stop laughing.

"I don't see what's so funny." Schramm seemed mildly affronted, though she wasn't sure which part had bothered him. Probably the butt-grab thing. Which reminded her of Trey being called the bandit assgrabber, and that made her laugh even harder.

She tried to explain as they hurried along, but between that and her laughter, all she managed was, "bandit assgrabber," which seemed to further annoy Schramm.

She tried to muffle her giggles, which resulted in a loud, extremely non-exec-worthy snort.

By the time they made it through a third maintenance corridor, she'd managed to compose herself, in spite of the amusement caused by the idea that another group of floor cleaners might pop out at them.

When they reached the end of that corridor, she turned to Schramm, wearing an almost straight face. "Two choices here. Short way is the courtyard, but it's out in the open and a risk. The other way is through the executive hallway and out a private entrance."

Schramm bit down on his bottom lip, in deep thought. "Better go with the courtyard. Execs will recognize me, and possibly you."

"Short and risky. I like it." She grinned at him, but he apparently hadn't yet forgiven her for the ass-grab thing.

"Okay," she said, "out we go. Watch the windows and roofs, but mostly, run like hell. Not in a straight line though, and not right against me."

"Corporations don't have snipers," he said, following her to the exit.

"We can hope." She threw the door open and ran way faster than anyone wearing an executive's suit ever had.

It was a nice courtyard, she noticed as she barreled

through it, edging to the side as long as she could to prevent from being as vulnerable on both sides. Eventually she had to leave it, though, and bolt straight for the designated meet-up entrance, where—if all had gone according to plan—the rest of the team awaited them.

A hot burning feeling shot down her leg. She'd pulled something. Well that was inconvenient. Then she realized that it felt different—she'd gotten shot.

Pulse pistols were close-range weapons, so the effect wasn't severe. She had no choice but to keep running, even though her left leg was rapidly going numb; her thigh down to her knee felt wooden.

Shit. She had twenty meters to go.

The numbness spread down toward her foot and she knew they weren't going to make it.

Suddenly the autovan came barreling into the courtyard. Trey leaned out a window and Tommy leaned out another. Both of them held large weapons, but she didn't have time to identify make and model.

"Down!" Trey bellowed.

Heedless of the autovan flying right at her, Reece locked up her knees and bent at the waist, causing her to eat dirt and go rolling. On the bright side, her left leg didn't feel a thing.

She sure hoped Schramm had gotten himself to the ground, to avoid whatever it was Trey wanted them to avoid.

On the other hand, the autovan hadn't veered away, and she had a sudden fear that death-by-autovan might end up being her epitaph.

Finally, the van slewed to the side and did a kind of miraculous skid that had it sliding into a turn that shielded her. Reece had landed on her arm and rolled off before turning her head to see Schramm several meters away from her, now also protected by the van.

The side door of the van flew open and she heard shots being fired, but she wasn't sure if they were coming at her or going toward the people who had already shot her. Probably some of both.

She got to her knees and tried to launch herself at the van, but only ended up going sprawling. Her left leg had gone not only numb, but now also refused to follow her commands. The knee just wouldn't tense, and she couldn't feel her foot.

Fine. Reece got back to her knees and started crawling forward on her one good leg.

Something caught her around the waist and she was about to attack when she realized it was Schramm lifting her to her feet and balancing her against him so she could hop on her good leg. He half-carried her to the van, where he unceremoniously dumped her in. Trey pulled her in further even as the van took off.

Reece heard the door slam as she pushed herself on the seat.

Ting ting ting. She heard things hitting the van, but they didn't seem like critical hits. More like someone throwing pebbles at them.

"How bad is it?" Trey asked, leaning down to examine her leg.

"Not sure. It's numb all the way down. I've never felt anything quite like it. Do you see any blood?"

"No. Wait. Yes."

"It's not just an energy blast, then." She didn't like that idea. Professional medical care wasn't in her immediate future. A bullet wound would be a big problem.

She had other problems at the moment, though. "Do we have everyone?"

Looking around, she counted heads. Yeah. Seven including her. Everyone accounted for.

"Anyone else injured?" she asked.

"Nothing serious," Trey answered. One of the others had passed an emergency medical kit to him. "We need to get your pants off."

"That's what all the guys say. In fact, when we were in there, you wouldn't believe what Schramm—" She'd been about to make a joke about Schramm being the new bandit assgrabber, but reality did a weird wobble and bounce around her. "I...I'm not good," she said.

Trey helped her lie down on the seat. "You're losing a lot of blood. I think an artery might have been hit. Don't try to stay conscious, okay? I'm going to look at this, and I'm no field medic. You'd probably be better off if you were out. Wait, here's an injection."

"No. Wait." She held up a hand to ward off the injection. "I need to know—did we get it? What went wrong?"

She heard Marky say, "I think we got it. We'll tell you the rest later. Just rest now."

She didn't feel the injection, but reality suddenly squinched together and everything went quiet.

MACHETE SYSTEM BOUNTY HUNTER – WITH GUNS BLAZING

RECOVERY

DATE: 06.01.8948 (Adjusted Gregorian)
LOCATION: Schramm's Farm, Agriculture Sector 43, Akonwara
REGION: Machete System, PED 4B, Orion Freedom Alliance

Reece felt like she was in a dark room, but she had no particular desire to see if that was true. She heard voices and they said words that she recognized, but they didn't string together any real meaning. Nothing worth struggling to hang on to and figure out, though.

She realized she'd had the sensation of being lifted and moved, and her head falling to the side, but she wasn't sure when that had happened.

Everything was still now, and that was good. She didn't like the words, which kept coming. She turned her head away, but that didn't quite work for some reason, so she just turned her whole self away and receded into the dark room.

* * * * *

Reece opened her eyes, feeling exhausted, though she knew she'd slept a long time. Maybe she'd stayed up too late. Wait. She didn't remember going to bed the night before. Why?

She had an odd sense of being out of sync with time. She felt kind of crappy and wanted to go back to sleep, but she was awake now. No going back.

Sighing, she sat up, then hissed. She pulled back the

sheet and saw bandages on her leg.

Her leg. Right. Trumark. The alarm. The courtyard.

Okay, it made sense now. How long ago had all that been, though? She didn't feel like it was the same day.

The ever-present starslight didn't help things. It could be two in the morning for all she knew.

Whatever the time, she was hungry and pushed the sheet away, swinging her legs over the edge of the bed.

The bathroom door opened and Kippy emerged.

"Whoa." He hurried over. "Careful. I didn't think you'd wake up while I was in the bathroom or I'd have had someone come sit with you."

"I'm hungry." Her voice sounded bad. Rough and raw.

He blinked at her, then laughed. "No 'where am I' or 'what day is it' or anything. Just 'I'm hungry.' Okay, then. What do you want? I'll see if we have it."

"We?" She looked around. This was the room she'd been using since arriving at Schramm's farmhouse. Was Kippy staying there now?

Well, sure, he probably was. They'd done an illegal thing, then she'd gotten shot. He wasn't going to just mosey back home after that.

Reece smiled at him.

He frowned. "Are you delirious or something? Why are you smiling?"

"Just glad you're here." Her voice sounded a little better the second time using it.

"Well, me too. In a way. And as for who all's here, it's pretty much all of us. The general idea was that they'd all go on holiday until we were sure no one had linked us to the hit on Trumark."

"How's that looking?" she asked.

"So far so good. But just because they aren't saying it doesn't mean they don't know it."

"Yeah. So how long has it been, then?"

"Two days. We called in a nurse Marky knew who was willing to make a call all the way out here and keep his mouth shut. Unfortunately, that meant no first-rate hospital care for you, so we kept you under to let you heal. Plus, you'll have a scar." He looked apologetic.

"Cool. Scars are badass. Like badges of honor."

He smiled. "Yeah?"

"Yeah. Well, a leg one, anyway. I'd be pissed if it were on my face."

"I kind of want to pretend there's one on your face, too, but that seems too mean," he admitted.

"Yeah. Good call on that one." She smeared her hands over her face. "Okay. So, last question. Did we get what we needed?"

He hesitated. "Mostly. Tell you what. You tell me what you want to eat, and we can talk about that after I've brought a tray for you."

"A tray? I can't just to sit at the table like a normal person?"

"If you want to. But wouldn't it be nicer if I brought it to you?" He smiled, and a dimple sank into his cheek.

She couldn't resist smiling back. "Yeah. It would."

"See? So what do you want?"

"Fried eggs on noodles. Rice. And a big ham sandwich, like this thick." She used her thumb and forefinger to indicate the width of her foot."

Kippy laughed. "You must be all better if you can eat all that. I don't know if we have it all, but I'll see what I can come up with."

He reached the door and paused. "Oh. Do you...I mean, you should have help getting up if you need to go...you know."

"Uh." She blinked. "I was kind of planning to shuffle to the bathroom once you were gone."

"How about I help you to the door?" he bargained.

"Okay."

He went over and put his arm around her waist to help her out of bed. She slid the right leg out first, which was fine. Then she moved the second one and it felt like someone else's leg. Twice its regular size and full of burning, aching pain.

"How does it feel?" he asked.

"Bad."

"Like, you can deal with it bad, or if I weren't here you'd be screaming kind of bad?"

"Somewhere in the middle," she admitted, "but closer to the dealing with it side."

He supported her while she cautiously made small steps toward the bathroom. The combination of wound and inactivity had her feeling stiff and weak.

She hated it. She needed to shake this off fast. "Okay. We've made it to the door. I shall now pee in privacy while you make me food."

He looked torn. "Are you sure you won't need help back to the bed?"

"I'll be okay. I just need to work out the stiffness." She gave him an encouraging smile.

"I'll be mad if you fall or something," he warned.

"I'm fine. Go. I'm starving."

He relented. "Okay. Just be careful, okay?"

She waved him off. Once he'd gone, she closed the door, making sure to move slowly and be cautious.

Without him there, she definitely felt less secure, but she was determined to prove that she was on the mend.

* * * * *

"You have delivered me nothing that I requested, other than the noodles." Reece surveyed her food curiously.

"We'll get a delivery today. We're a little low, since the place wasn't stocked to feed so many people. That Tommy eats a whole lot more than you'd think." Kippy sat next to her bed, watching her.

She took a bite of noodles. "They're good."

The rest was a strange hodgepodge of sliced cheese, pickled radishes, and a plain tortilla.

"You owe me a sandwich, though," she added.

"Sure. We'll have a sandwich date as soon as we get back home." He said it easily with a smile, but Reece had to wonder at the technical definition of his use of the word 'date.'

Did he mean they'd go grab some food to stuff in their faces at an appointed time, or did he mean a *date* kind of date?

Was it bad if she wanted it to be a date kind of date? Would that risk screwing things up for them forever?

"Sandwiches are good." Sure, it was a lame thing to

say, but it was all she had that was suitably unrevealing.

Casually, she switched topics. "Have you checked in on Aunt Ruth and Dex?"

"Yeah. They're fine."

She twirled up some more noodles. "Did you tell the others I'm awake?"

"Nope. I wanted to give you a chance to eat first. Once they know you're awake, they'll come flooding in here to see for themselves.

"Think so?" She rather liked the idea of all those people caring about her wellbeing.

"I know so."

"Okay, then. Fill me in on what happened with you guys and what information we got. I'm a little mad that Schramm and I didn't have a chance to do more than serve as a minor distraction." She frowned.

She sat up straighter. "And you know what else? I don't even know where my milkshake went. I had it, then I didn't. It must have gotten dropped somewhere."

That reminded her of knocking the milkshake out of Schramm's hands, and she giggled. She'd tell Kippy that story later, as she didn't want to get distracted. "So what did we get?"

He watched her, shaking his head. "Wow, it's like you're having a whole conversation with yourself. It must be exhausting inside your head. Okay. The first part of it went off fine. Marky and Raya conned their way in. Not too surprising. Raya met her objectives and got Marky to the right place, where she got into the system and started pulling down the necessary data. We've been looking at what she got, and it's some good stuff. The unfortunate part is that it's mostly circumstantial. There's no dead-on proof. The alarm went off before we could get that."

Reece groaned, frustrated. "What caused the alarm to go off?"

Kippy handed her a napkin, which she took as a hint that she had food on her face, so she wiped her mouth.

He said, "They apparently implemented random periodic reauthentication. I bet it's a real pain in the butt for people who work there, but every so often, everyone has to log back into their accounts in order to continue working. Marky didn't expect that, and she was about a second and a half too late in coming up with the reauthentication code."

She sighed. "So close. Now what? Does Schramm have another idea?"

"Actually, yes, thanks to what Marky found."

She paused with a forkful of noodles halfway to her mouth. "Really? What is it?"

"I'm not sure. He's keeping us as uninformed as possible, in case we do get caught. If we're simple contractors who didn't know anything, it'll go much better for us."

She nodded. "Yeah. I'm glad he's being careful. I don't want any of you to end up in trouble because of this."

He shrugged. "We've all assumed the risk via our own free will. We want to help you, and to do that, it would be best if we knew more."

"It may come to that, depending on what happens next. We're limited in who we can ask for help."

"Way to make me feel like second choice."

She looked up quickly, but his eyes were crinkled with humor. "It's not that. You're my first choice. I just don't want you getting hurt because of me."

"I know. But if I were in trouble, you'd be right in front, stepping in front of bullets and stuff, right? Don't even say you wouldn't because I know better."

"That's different."

"What," he pressed, "because this is what you do for a living? Don't think I've ever been thrilled about it. But it's what you want, and so that's the end of it. This time, I'm insisting that this is what *I* want. And that's the end of it. Okay?"

She studied him and saw total conviction in the slant of his eyebrows and the lines around his mouth.

He wasn't going to budge this time.

"Okay. You're in, then."

He looked surprised. "I kind of thought you'd put up more of a fight."

"I can see you're serious. Plus, my noodles are getting cold." She slurped some up, just to make her point. She paused. "Plus, you're awfully cute."

He brightened. "I am?"

Had she just said that? It must be whatever medication they'd given her.

She stuffed her mouth with more noodles.

* * * * *

"This has not been my week, health-wise." Reece grimaced as she hobbled across the farmhouse's living room. Fortunately, it was big enough to hold six people. With no promise of imminent mayhem, Tommy had gone back to tend his shop. He'd turned out to be very helpful in their escape from Trumark, and Reece was grateful. He'd made her promise to call him when there were more people to shoot at.

She was surprised that the others hadn't returned home. They all had jobs. But here they were, hanging out in the farmhouse, plotting on retaliating against Cooper Fields.

"Any better?" Marky gave Reece a sympathetic smile.

"Everything except the leg is just fine. What did they shoot me with, anyway? Razor blades?"

"Standard ammo," Trey said. "It just always hurts more to get shot than people think."

Reece made a scoffing sound and sat on the chair he vacated for her. He squeezed in next to Raya, even though there was a hardback chair on the other side of the room.

No doubt he'd claim the couch was more comfortable, which it was, but Reece knew that was just an excuse to get close to his new girlfriend.

"It'll be another day or two before I'm getting around like normal," she said. It would still probably hurt, but she didn't have time to waste on healing.

She didn't mind waiting on old-fashioned healing. Not as much as someone who hadn't grown up doing it out of necessity, anyway. Though given the choice, she'd have a hospital do most of the healing for her.

"So fill me in on what we got, what we didn't, and what our new objective is," she said. "I'm sure we're all disappointed that the Trumark hit didn't get us everything we need, like we'd hoped, but at least we got out alive and not too badly harmed."

Schramm said, "We got enough information to know what we need to do next, along with exactly where we can find that information. It's a shame we couldn't get it from Trumark, but there's another place."

Reece nodded. "Okay."

"The good news is that we'll know exactly what we're getting into, since it's familiar," Schramm continued.

"Are you saying what I think you're saying?" Reece squinted at him.

Schramm nodded.

A riot of conflicting emotions ricocheted through her. "We're going to infiltrate Rexcare's headquarters."

"It seems fitting, I think, since our problems began there. Why shouldn't they end there, as well?" Schramm wore a determined expression.

Why? Well, because they had strong security even on a regular day, but no doubt, Cooper Fields was on alert and would have additional safeguards. Compared to getting into Rexcare, their busting into Trumark would seem like a wee prank. A warm-up for the real thing.

She looked around the room at all the faces. Schramm, Trey, Raya, Marky, Apolla, and Kippy. They were all committed to this, and they were risking a lot.

It was scary. Reece had always done her job on her own, a sole entity of corporate justice. Now she had not only a partner, but a whole team of people she cared about. Some of them she cared a *lot* about.

And yet...the idea of the challenge of getting into

Rexcare, and the satisfaction she'd get when they pulled it off, excited her. A lot.

Reece took a deep breath. "Okay. Let's figure out how we'll do this."

* * * * *

The solution to Cooper Field's sabotage, as they determined it to be, was a three-pronged approach.

Step One: Hit Rexcare. Get the info.

Step Two: Refuse to be removed from the building. Hole up. Fight back.

Step Three: Get the information to the board. Insist that they recognize Cooper Fields' machinations and dismiss him, return Schramm, Reece, and Trey to their regular positions and see that any criminal charges against the others were dropped.

What a lot of effort just to return things to the way they'd been.

Secretly, Reece also had intentions of getting even with Cooper Fields once everything had been set right, but she didn't share that with the others. They'd try to dissuade her, and she had no intentions of being dissuaded. Someone who had caused her friends so much difficulty simply had to be dealt with.

Plus, he'd inconvenienced her, too. Feeding him a revenge sandwich was a duty she couldn't neglect.

When Schramm, Reece, Marky, and Apolla put their heads together, they came up with a comprehensive tactical plan to get into the headquarters building, get to where they needed to be, access the information and download it, and get that information to the board.

The rest should pretty much take care of itself.

"I'm going to have to pull in some favors for this," Apolla said, frowning at the schematics they had sketched out on the table. "I'm set up to do surveillance from the exterior. Doing it from the inside, and slapping it together when we get there, will require some hardware I don't have."

"Is it that different, exterior and interior?" Reece asked.

Apolla nodded, deep in thought. "Similar concepts, in general, but different approaches. "

Marky ran her fingers through her short, spiked pale-blonde hair. "My job's pretty much the same, whether inside or out, but cracking Rexcare will be easier thanks to what you two have given me. But I could speed things up if I got some new hardware, too."

"A few seconds could mean the difference between success and failure, so whatever will buy us time, we have to do." Schramm looked from Marky to Apolla. "Cooper will be looking for us, but other than that, waiting a day or two to get the supplies we need won't make any difference. He'll already know about us busting into Trumark."

"At least he doesn't know what we got," Marky said. "Since I was able to hide that."

"Right." Schramm clapped his hands together, making a surprisingly loud crack. "Figure out what you need, where you can get it, how long it will take, and report back."

He ducked his head. "Er…I mean please. I forgot for a

second that we weren't in a board room and you aren't my employees."

Reece had never expected to see Schramm embarrassed. It was kind of cute, in the sense that she'd rarely seen him uncertain about anything. Every now and then, she saw past the veneer of executive persona and saw a real person underneath.

Marky's eyes seemed to linger on Schramm, and Reece wondered if she was thinking the same thing.

Maybe not. Marky hadn't known him until recently, so she had no prior understanding of him to compare his current behavior with. She was probably just curious about him.

Or maybe…

Nah. Executives weren't Marky's type. She liked her men a lot more capricious and unpredictable.

Silly thought.

"I guess that leaves me without a job for once," Reece said, not feeling a bit bad about it. Considering the fact that she'd gotten shot and gone through the pain of having her Link jailbroken, she'd already done a lot of the heavy lifting on this venture. If others could pitch in, all the better.

She'd contribute in a simpler way. "I'll make some lunch.'

In the kitchen, she assembled a bounty of fresh ingredients and began chopping and peeling. As she sliced carrots, Kippy came in.

"Look at you, pretending you can cook," he teased, standing behind her and peeking over her shoulder.

"I can so. Look. I'm cooking."

"Nuh uh," he chuckled. "Cooking involves heat and changing ingredients from one form into another. What you're doing is preparing."

"It's the same thing." She paused and made a shooing gesture over her shoulder without looking back at him.

"Is not," he argued.

"Is too. Stop that or I won't let you have any."

"Give me a bite of carrot and I'll quit," he promised.

"Fine." She picked up a slice of the purple vegetable and turned to hand it to him, but he leaned down, mouth opening.

Feeling a little weird about it, she put the piece of carrot in his mouth. Her fingers grazed his lips and she was suddenly aware that they were stomach to stomach, with her back against the countertop.

Kippy chewed slowly and swallowed, his gaze not leaving hers.

Reece's hand suddenly seemed homeless, hanging in midair. She rested it gingerly against his chest. The air felt thick and she reached for some words to cut through it. "That kiss, a little while back. We never talked about it."

"That's true." He put his hands on her waist. "We didn't."

"Was it just spontaneous, or did it...mean something?"

"What do you think?"

"I think it means something." She had to look away to be able to say it.

"I think you're right."

She was about half a breath away from throwing

caution to the wind and going for a repeat performance, but instead made a last-ditch effort to remain objective. "But what if—"

Raya's voice pierced the moment. "Do we still have any tea? I'm—" She broke off abruptly. "Oh. Sorry."

Reece's cheeks tingled and she returned to cutting carrots. "You'll need to brew it, but we have lots.

Kippy moved away and pulled a large pitcher off a shelf. "I can help. Especially since I was the one that finished off the last of the tea this morning."

Reece's cheeks cooled as she finished slicing the carrots and moved on to some avocadoes. She sneaked a glance at Kippy, who seemed entirely at ease filling the pitcher with ice and handing Raya a stirring spoon.

It felt strange having that kind of chemistry with Kippy. And kind of…nice. And worrying.

Worst of all, she'd caught herself wishing Raya hadn't interrupted them.

She started slicing onions with a vengeance.

PICKING FRUIT

DATE: 06.01.8948 (Adjusted Gregorian)
LOCATION: Schramm's Farm, Agriculture Sector 43, Akonwara
REGION: Machete System, PED 4B, Orion Freedom Alliance

After lunch, everyone played King Sweep. Not surprisingly, with Marky around, somehow they started betting. Reece bowed out when real money became involved, but with Trey being such a good player, Schramm turning out to be remarkably good at it, and Marky being Marky, the game heated up fast.

Kippy stayed in the game but tended to fold early before the pot got too big. He didn't seem to mind that the stakes were too high for his comfort. He'd never been much of a gambler, though he did enjoy games.

Apolla remained in the game for several hands, but after losing big in a particularly tense round, she threw in her cards and opted for watching the others play.

"I'm going to go sit on the porch," Reece said. "Anyone want to join me?"

Apolla shrugged. "Some fresh air might be nice."

Raya looked at Reece, then looked at her cards. "I fold. I'll come too."

Outside, Reece and Raya sat on the porch swing while Apolla settled into a heavy rocking chair.

Raya took a long, deep breath. "It's nice out here. Makes me think of growing fruit trees."

"I had the same thought," Reece admitted. "Though living out here would have its drawbacks. No nightlife, and having groceries delivered would get expensive fast. But if you went to get them in person, you'd spend all day doing it."

"I guess that's why Schramm has the autovan," Apolla said.

"Not that he's out here much," Reece pointed out. "Doesn't that seem like a waste?"

"Yeah." Raya shook her head. "Having something really great and never using it." A mischievous expression shifted her mouth into a tiny grin. "Kind of like you and Kippy."

Reece gasped theatrically. At least, it was mostly for theatrical effect. "What is that supposed to mean?" she demanded lightly.

"I know what I saw earlier. And I know what I've been seeing with you two. Sneaking glances at each other, all those soft expressions. What's with you two?"

"It's complicated," Reece said.

"People always say that." Apolla tilted her head to the side, looking thoughtful. "But you know what, it almost never is. Be together or don't be together. It's pretty simple."

"But we've been friends almost all our lives. What if being together messes that up?" Reece wasn't accustomed to talking about such a highly personal subject, but it was apparently no secret anyway.

"What if it doesn't?" Raya countered. "And what if you don't go for it, and all the tension ruins your friendship anyway? I mean, how would you feel if he started dating someone else? Would you want to hang out like always?"

Reece tried to imagine it and had a bad feeling in the pit of her stomach. "I don't love that idea," she admitted.

"So there you go," Raya said, swiped her hands together as if brushing dust off them. "Problem solved."

Apolla sat upright from her sprawled position, her eyes wide. "You know what I just thought of?"

"What?" Reece had a feeling she wouldn't like it.

"If Raya goes in there and whispers something in Trey's ear, the game would probably fall apart, and then Kippy would need something to do."

"And?" Reece asked.

Apolla said, "I could mention that you'd gone for a walk in the orchard. If he came and joined you, wouldn't that be romantic?"

"Probably, if it weren't like a thousand degrees out," Reece said.

Apolla deflated. "Oh. Right. I guess bees and excessive sweating aren't very romantic. Damn."

Reece laughed. "Plus, walking isn't fun right now. Thanks for the thought, though."

Raya slid off the swing and gave them a wink. "I like the idea of getting Trey's attention, though. I'll see you two later."

Apolla rocked slowly back and forth. "It would seem we're short on guys. The two I'd consider are already taken."

"What about Schramm?" Reece asked.

"Oh. I mean, he's nice, and not bad-looking, but he's a little clean-cut for me." Apolla shrugged. "I prefer highly exciting, very short-lived whirlwind relationships."

Reece grinned. "I see."

"I think my expectations are too high," Apolla confided. "I want all the exciting stuff from the beginning, without all the boring stuff that it all settles into. I'll probably get over that eventually."

"You haven't found any guys worth keeping around long term?" Reece asked.

"Nah. The sad truth is that I'm attracted to assholes, and they can only hide their stink for a very limited amount of time."

Reece blinked, too startled for a moment to react. Then she burst out laughing. "Wow, what a way to put it! Very succinct. It's good you know yourself, though."

Apolla grinned. "I've never been accused of not having a strong opinion. And on that note, I think I'll take a shower and get to bed."

"Is it that late?" Reece checked her chronometer and found that it had become late evening. That game of King Sweep had occupied them all for quite some time.

The persimmons that had been almost ripe two days ago were ready to eat. Since she wasn't tired, she might as well go check. On her way off the porch, she grabbed a bushel basket just in case she found some fruit to bring back.

Walking slowly and carefully, she passed through the garden and its fresh, fragrant smells. She took in long lungfuls as she strolled by. When she got to the trees, their shade eased some of the heat pounding down on her.

Reece found a few apples that were ready to pick, so she grabbed them before they could drop to the ground and get bruised. She could see more ripe ones hanging heavy higher up, but they were too far out of her reach.

Carrying the basket with the apples, she kept going until she got to the persimmon trees. The fruit were ripe, all right. Brown in color, they looked more like tomatoes, but she knew how ripe and sweet these would be.

She plucked them off the tree, two by two, gently placing them in the basket. When she'd covered the bottom of the basket, she lifted it to test its weight. She had no intention of struggling to carry back an overly heavy basket. Not only would she sweat like crazy, it would be tough on her leg, which still twinged with every step.

As she was stretching to reach a particularly large fruit, she heard someone coming. She pulled the persimmon free and turned.

Kippy watched her curiously. "It's kind of funny to see you out in the country, doing country things." He pointed to her cut-off shorts and tank top. "Wearing country things."

She looked down at the shorts, which had recently been pants. She hadn't had much selection in clothing, and the pants she'd worn to Trumark had gotten damaged anyway, so cutting them had been a no-brainer.

"I've worn a lot worse," she said. "Remember when we used to get hand-me-downs from wherever we could get them?"

He laughed. "I remember wearing girls' shirts during the winter when I was twelve. I was not pleased."

She giggled. "You always made anything look cool. Some of the other boys started wearing girl sweaters that year, as I recall."

"I know how to work it." He posed like a fashion model.

He was trying to be goofy, but in fact, he looked awfully good. Reece's amusement dried up. She took a bite of the persimmon in her hand to cover up her sudden shift in emotions.

"Is that a tomato?" He stepped closer. "That's a weird way to eat that."

"Persimmon," she said around a mouthful of fruit. "Here." She held it out to him.

Kippy took it, but then moved closer again. "You have juice on your mouth." He brushed it away with his thumb but came closer still.

Why did she feel frozen? The heat seemed to have glued Reece in place.

Kippy leaned down and gave her a long kiss that was even sweeter than the fruit. Reece heard the persimmon drop to the ground as he put his arms around her.

If she'd had any doubts before, she didn't now. She'd somehow fallen completely, helplessly in love with her best friend. When had that happened, exactly? Why was she only finding out now?

Kippy lifted his head slightly, cupping her face in his hands.

"What are we doing?" she whispered.

"You already know," he answered softly.

"Well...why now?"

"Because you were too dumb to figure it out a year ago when I figured it out." He smiled. "So I had to wait."

"Wait, a year ago?" She leaned back slightly to get a

better look at his face.

He looked sheepish. "Janice and I didn't break up because we had different goals. It was because as great as she was, I always wanted to be with you instead. When I really thought about what that meant, it started to fall into place."

"Wow." She flexed her fingers on his back, just because she could. "This is weird."

"But a nice kind, right?"

"Oh, yeah," she agreed quickly. "Really…good."

He laughed and picked her up to spin her around.

She squeaked. "Ow! Dammit! My leg."

"Oh! Right." He froze in place and adjusted his hold on her to relieve the pressure on her leg. "Sorry."

"That was really stupid," she said, her leg aching.

He stared at her with guilt and concern, looking so stricken that she laughed.

"What, you're joking?" he asked, perplexed.

"No. You totally mashed my bad leg. But the look on your face…. You're too cute."

He grimaced. "Cute? That is not what I've spent the last year hoping you'd see in me."

"Handsome," she corrected herself quickly. "No, gorgeous."

He didn't seem entirely convinced, so she added, "Hot."

Kippy grinned. "There you go. That's the one." He kissed her again, still holding her close.

Reece heard something moving in the trees and quickly pulled away, looking.

"What?" Kippy looked to his left and right, searching.

"Nothing. Just the breeze. I thought someone was coming this way, probably to kick our asses. That's just kind of been how my luck has been going lately."

Kippy set her back on her feet, taking care to balance her until her sore leg was securely positioned. "A guy might take offense at that, present circumstances considered."

She grinned. "I mean outside of right this moment, my luck hasn't been running all that great."

"Eh. Take what you can get." He grinned and elbowed her.

She faked an offended huff, bent to pick up the fallen persimmon and tossed it at him. She pantomimed a forceful throw, but then lobbed it so that it barely bumped him before falling on the ground.

He stared at her in mock outrage. "How dare you? I'm going to have to wash these pants now."

"Aw, that's too bad," she teased. "I know how you hate wearing clean clothes."

"Oh, that is it!" he declared, lunging for a fallen, mushy persimmon.

Reece shrieked and dashed for a tree as fast as her leg would let her without aching too much. She hid behind the trunk then peeked around.

The persimmon hit the tree just below her chin with a sharp *thwack*.

"You really threw that!" she objected. "I just pretended."

"You started it."

Another persimmon hit the tree.

"Oh. Now you've done it. It is *on*. No one throws

overripe fruit at me and gets away with it." Reece bent and gathered up two persimmons that lay at her feet.

A fruity projectile hit her in the butt.

"Bring it," he taunted. "It'll end the same way the great battle of the uneaten sandwiches did when we were twelve."

"Aunt Ruth grounded me for that, you know," she said, peeking around the tree and tossing a persimmon in his direction.

"I remember."

Two more fruits hit the tree.

He added, "You'll be grounded this time, too."

She laughed at his trash talk. "Automatic disqualification for a bad pun. And you know what else? Your aim sucks."

She stood and threw three fruits at him in quick succession. One of them glanced off his arm and another hit him square in the chest.

She felt a hit on her left leg and she bent to grasp it. "My leg!"

"Oh crap! Sorry!" He started toward her.

"Sucker!" She grabbed two fruits and threw them as she straightened.

He yelled in surprise, then, laughing, ran at her.

Reece ran as fast as her leg would let her, trying to put a big oak tree between them. Then she changed her mind and slowed down to let Kippy catch her.

It was about time she did that. Especially since she now felt like, whatever happened with them, they'd still be best friends.

*****

Two days later, Reece's leg was almost back to normal, and Marky and Apolla had gotten together what they needed.

It was time to make their stand.

In spite of what she'd said to Kippy on the day of their persimmon battle, Reece felt pretty fortunate that Cooper Fields hadn't found them in the meantime, hanging out at Schramm's farmhouse. Clearly, he'd done very well indeed at hiding his hideout's ownership

Maybe their luck was changing. If so, there couldn't be a better time for it. Even though they'd meticulously planned their assault on Rexcare, there was still a lot that could go wrong.

She mentally slapped her brain. Nope. Nothing was going to go wrong. Everything would go as planned, they'd get the info, restore Schramm's reputation, and life would go on as usual.

From the window of the living room, Reece saw Kippy helping Trey load up the autovan.

Well, life wouldn't go on *exactly* as usual. Some parts, hopefully, would get a whole lot better.

Though she'd been comfortable in her cutoff shorts and tank top, it felt good to be back in what she considered to be her work uniform—her black pants and red and black jacket. Most importantly, she wore a full complement of weaponry.

Kippy and Trey had spent the previous day painting the van to look like a delivery vehicle from Rexcare's preferred package delivery service. The red stripes on a gold background looked garish to Reece, but the van appeared to be the real thing. Kippy had been better at his after-school job at the paint shop than she'd ever realized.

Reece carried out a bag with food for them to eat on the way, and Schramm closed the door to the farmhouse behind them.

Reece had hoped she'd be able to come back one day, but not too soon. She was done with hiding.

It took them most of the day to get to the chop shop Marky had directed them to. Once there, the team pulled out the back two rows of seating and replaced them with cargo racks. They arranged the cargo racks so that they'd conceal the people hiding away inside.

While they got the van ready, Apolla loaded her equipment into a large backpack. After shrugging it onto her back, she came to wish the others luck.

"It should take me twenty-five minutes to get to my colleague's place from here," she said. "I'll check in with you once I've arrived."

Reece nodded. Apolla had made a deal with another surveillance specialist to use his setup. It hadn't been cheap, and he'd likely be able to figure out what they'd done after the fact, but by then it wouldn't matter if he knew. It was too bad Apolla couldn't use her own place, but going there would be too risky as Trumark had likely identified her as one of the people who had hacked their system.

"Okay. Stay alert and..." Reece stopped herself. "I was going to tell you to try to avoid cameras but look at who I'm talking to."

Apolla smirked. "Right. And I'd tell you to be careful but look who I'm talking to."

Reece grinned. "I'm always careful. Making it look like I'm making things up as I go along is just part of my mystique."

"Yeah, right," Apolla scoffed. "Anyway, I'll be in touch soon. Good luck."

"You too."

Reece watched her go, then helped the others finish loading the van. She hoped Apolla got to her destination without trouble. If they didn't have her helping them, this would never work.

* * * * *

Reece almost started to rethink their plan when her knees were shoved up to her chin with her arms wrapped around them, her back pressed into Trey's side. Worse, the air in the back of the van wasn't circulating, and it was getting way too hot.

She doubted Trey, Schramm, and Marky were any more comfortable, so she didn't bother complaining, even though she could have done it silently with Schramm or Trey via the Link. But Schramm had other things on his mind and Trey would probably just make fun of her.

"Here we go," Kippy said.

The movement of the vehicle stopped and Reece held her breath.

Someone said something, but it was too muffled for her to make out.

"Delivery for the maintenance department." Kippy's voice was clear and sounded carefree.

The voice said something apologetic.

"Uh, there's a lot here. That would take me a while. There isn't someone who can help?" Now Kippy sounded quite put out.

Schramm had pinpointed a time after the daytime intake department had left for the day but before the nighttime maintenance team had arrived, leaving the delivery bays unoccupied. It was that tiny window of opportunity that had spawned this entire strategy.

"Yeah, I know, it's not your fault." Kippy sounded resigned. "This is going to take me a while, though."

After a few more muffled words, the autovan moved forward again.

They'd cleared the first hurdle.

<We're in,> Reece said to Apolla, hoping she had some good news for them.

Apolla responded quickly. As soon as she'd gotten to her destination, she would have gone right into pulling up as much surveillance as she could. <I'm standing by. As soon as you get that threadjacker in place, I'll be able to view Rexcare's internal feeds. I'm ready.>

<I'm ready, too. Shouldn't be long now.>

<Understood.>

The back doors opened and Kippy began moving boxes out of the way to let Reece and the others out. They kept their backs against the van and slid out along the side away from the dock, where they wouldn't be in plain view with the van in the way.

Reece sent Raya a message. <We're in. You're up.>

At the front of the building, Raya sat in a taxi, pretending to be occupied with a call until Reece gave her the go-ahead. They hadn't wanted to put the threadjacker in place if they hadn't made it into the delivery area, because in exactly fifty-four minutes, the system would do a check for new devices and find the threadjacker.

<Just entered the lobby.>

As an employee of Donnercorp, Raya shouldn't be viewed with suspicion. There was some concern that she'd been identified at Trumark, but two days of monitoring corporate feeds had led them to believe Raya wasn't a suspect.

At least, Reece hoped so.

She imagined Raya charming the desk staff and gaining access to the building. Reece didn't know how she'd do it, but she was certain she would.

People rarely said no to Raya.

At the back of the autovan, Kippy slowly loaded boxes onto a conveyer in the receiving bay, careful not to finish the job too quickly.

Reece counted down the minutes.

Raya responded on an open channel they had with all the others. <I've got access to the second floor. What's my best option here?>

Second floor? Reece didn't waste time asking what lie she'd told to get past the lobby without an appointment or an escort, but she wondered about it. The second floor was mostly conference rooms, so maybe she'd claimed to be meeting up with someone.

<First conference room on your right,> Schramm

answered. *<There's an access node for sim conferencing. Plant it there, then find a place to hide and wait.>*

Trey had made an argument for Raya leaving the building afterward, but if she could remain undetected, or at least unsuspected, she could be useful to them in accessing other parts of the Rexcare HQ.

A few minutes later, Raya indicated that she was in the conference room. Everyone waited with bated breath, hoping for good news, when she spoke again. <*I have a problem. The device I have has a different kind of port than the connection.>*

Apolla immediately asked, <What does the connection look like?>

Raya answered, <Kind of bulgy in the middle, and the ends taper.>

<Okay. Do you see a rectangular box about the size of your fist?>

<Yes,> Raya said.

<Take the cable out of it and attach it to the device I gave you. Then you'll be able to plug it in.> Apolla's instructions came incredibly fast, like she didn't even have to think about it.

<Okay. It's in.>

<Now just turn it on,> Apolla said. A moment later, she said, <I've got it. Feeds are coming from all over the building. Give me a minute to get a read on it all.>

Leaning against the van, Reece let out a small breath of relief. Everything hinged on Apolla leading them through the building. Reece's heart had frozen over for a moment when Raya had said she couldn't connect Apolla's device.

<Okay,> Apolla said. <I can see you. Take that closest doorway and go left. Quickly. No one's there.>

Schramm, Trey, Marky and Reece hurried toward the door.

Reece's heart raced. Finally, she got to actually do something.

Her gaze collided for just a moment with Kippy's as she entered the building. There was no time for him to wish her luck, but that was okay. She knew he was thinking it. He'd finish unloading the truck.

In a twist of rough justice and pragmatism, they'd packed their recyclable trash into the boxes to give them some weight, and also relieve Schramm of having to have it hauled away. She didn't have time to laugh about it, though, as they followed Apolla's instructions.

<Left here. Wait. Now, the office at the end of the hall. Hang on. Okay. The elevator door is open. Go!>

They hurried to the elevator and pressed the 'door close' button.

<Looking good,> Apolla said. <I'm recording the bits you're about to travel through and replaying that feed on a loop while you do your thing.>

<That should work unless someone suddenly appears on camera when you kill the recording,> Schramm said.

<Give me a little credit,> Apolla answered. <I'm watching each one to make sure no one's there when I flip the feed back to live.>

<My apologies,> Schramm told her. <I'm going to have to offer you a job, apparently.>

<Yeah, you are,> she agreed. <But I'm not sure you can afford me.>

The elevator stopped and the doors opened.

"Ready?" Trey asked Marky.

"Yep."

"You'll only have sixty seconds to get past the login. Otherwise, we'll be caught," Schramm reminded.

Marky nodded, her expression tense but determined.

<Go now!> Apolla said.

They rushed off the elevator, down the hall, and toward the data center that Reece had recently unofficially accessed to get contract information she wasn't supposed to have.

It had been necessary then, and it was necessary now.

Schramm and Marky entered the data center, while Reece and Trey stationed themselves outside it. They were the last line of defense, should the worst happen.

Reece hoped the worst didn't happen.

As Marky and Schramm began doing what they had to do, Trey looked at Reece. "Think they'll get it?"

"I wouldn't be here if I didn't think we'd be successful." She gave him a dirty look for questioning the outcome.

He linked her into a message with Raya and Kippy. <How are things out there? We've made it to the target and Marky's doing her thing.>

Kippy answered first. <Nothing happening out here. Well, other than a hot dog vendor who keeps giving me weird looks.>

<So buy a hot dog.> Reece said. <You'll seem less suspicious.>

Kippy snorted before answering, <Those hot dogs are what's suspicious. Who knows what's in there, and whether it

will make me sick.>

Raya's sent them a message. <*Sorry. Got caught up in a conversation about some sports team. I had to pretend I can't get enough loofball.>*

<*Lootball,>* Reece corrected her. <*Where are you?>*

<*Fourth floor, near accounting.>*

<*Why there?>* Trey asked.

<*Because I don't belong here and I have to pretend I do. Every time I run into someone, I have to make up a new lie about why I'm here and they helpfully escort me somewhere. I'm like the baton at a relay race or something.>*

Trey said, <*I don't think that analogy's accurate. Anyway, where are you going now?>*

<*Restroom. I've gone to one three times already, but it's the one place people can't be suspicious about me wanting to find. Hang on. Here comes another one.>* Raya went silent.

Reece looked over her shoulder, into the small window in the door. She saw Marky bent over a sim and Schramm standing beside her, frowning.

She'd always wondered about that window. It was tiny—about the size of her hands if she made an L-shape with each and put her thumbs end to end. There were no windows in the walls, which was for security purposes, no doubt. So why have one in the door? The only explanation she could think of was that some executive had gotten annoyed at having to open the door to see if someone was in there.

Or maybe it was there for security to peek into and make sure no one was there? Probably not. Rexcare didn't really have roving security guards of that type. They had people in the lobby, outside the lobby, and in the entryways of the bottom floor. All the access points, for the most part.

<Um, guys?> Raya said via the group Link. <Someone just went running through here. Literally running.>

<Apolla?> Reece asked.

<Looking. Okay. There. Yeah. Well, that's not good. Marky, have you been detected? It looks like people are headed your way.>

<Not that I know of,> Marky said. <I'm downloading the proof now. It's going to take another full minute.>

<You don't have time,> Apolla said. <I estimate these two will reach you in about fifty seconds, if they take a security elevator.>

Reece had ridden in one of those once. It involved locking your feet into clamps in the floor and holding on to the wall handles. It also involved not hanging onto your lunch. She'd never ridden one again.

<Which elevator?> Raya asked.

<Twelve west.>

Raya said, <I'm on it. I'll buy you the time.>

<How?> Schramm asked.

Raya didn't answer.

Trey looked worried, no doubt for more than one reason. "We should get ready."

Reece reached into her weapon belt and pulled out small tablet-sized circles. She ran down one side of the hall, sticking them to the wall, then doubled back and did the same against the wall in the other direction. The flashbangs were tiny, but powerful. They'd briefly blind and deafen anyone who happened to be right by them when they were activated.

Reece pulled up the control panel for them and slid it to the right of her vision. She checked her chronometer against the time stamp of Raya's last message.

Fifty seconds.

Fifty-five.

Reece held her breath.

Sixty!

She threw the door open and propped it that way with her heel. "Do you have it?" She shouted in over her shoulder, briefly taking her eyes off the hallway.

Trey stood tense, his hands on his Rikulf Specials.

"Got it!" Marky shouted, yanking something out of a machine and stuffing it in her pocket. "Let's go!"

Reece's heart leapt. They had it. They'd gotten the proof they needed to make all of this end and let life go back to normal.

<*I couldn't keep them any longer,*> Raya reported. <*They're on their way to you. I count seven...no, eight.*>

The team just had to get the proof to the board now, but they had to avoid getting grabbed by security in the meantime. If they got caught, their proof would be lost and they'd have no more chances. They'd look guiltier than they had to start with.

<*First objective reached!*> Schramm announced on the shared channel. <*Moving on to stage two.*>

Apolla sent a message. <*Bad news. It looks like all of security has been alerted. There's a small army coming your way.*>

Reece looked at Trey. They'd hoped to get the proof and immediately hand it over to the board while remaining in the building. No chance of that now.

They led Schramm and Apolla back the way they'd come, then took a sharp left turn. Reece activated the flashbangs as soon as they were past them.

"We can't use the elevators," she said. "We're not going to be able to get out of here. We have to go to Plan B."

"There's a Plan B?" Trey said.

"It's not a good one," Reece admitted, pointing to her left to indicate another turn ahead.

Behind them, the flashbangs started going off.

"Marky," she said, pointing ahead. "That door. We need it open, like now."

"I should be able to get it." As she ran, Marky reached into the bag on her shoulder and pulled out a white, rubbery-looking glove. She pulled it on her right hand and it seemed to conform to her skin.

Marky put her hand on the scanner, then jammed a chip stick into the dataport. "I've got the base logarithm for the code on here. It just needs a few seconds to find the right parameters."

The hall behind them had gone quiet after the flashbangs, but Reece heard footsteps coming quickly their way.

"How long?" Trey asked.

A bleep sound indicated success. Marky yanked the door open and they ran inside, slamming the door behind them and locking it.

Trey reached out and crushed the emergency release tube with his bare hand.

"They won't be able to get in now," Schramm said, looking around the large machine-room. "The trouble is, we also can't get out."

BOLT HOLE
DATE: 06.04.8948 (Adjusted Gregorian)
LOCATION: Rexcare HQ, Ohiyo, Akonwara
REGION: Machete System, PED 4B, Orion Freedom Alliance

"That's not exactly true," Reece said. "They can get in via the air coolant system, if they tear up some of the ceiling panels. Then they can drop down on us."

"Can we get out that way?" Marky asked, breathing heavily.

They were all breathing a little hard.

"No." Reece looked up at the two-story height of the room. "Too high, and we don't have the tools to cut through the metal."

"So we're stuck until they get to us," Schramm said.

"Yes, but we have two things going for us," Reece said.

"What?" Marky asked.

Reece didn't immediately answer Marky's question. She looked at Trey. "Those eyes of yours. Can you upload a direct visual to a live Link feed?"

Reece's own Link allowed her to establish real-time visual contact for speaking to someone, but that had no recording abilities. Alternatively, she could record what she saw and upload it, but it would take longer.

"Yes," he said. "Why?"

Marky rummaged in her bag and handed Trey a reader device. Then she handed him the data stick she'd taken from the server room. "Because you're going to read this and broadcast it to the board. And if they don't respond before Cooper Fields' people get to us, you'll put it out on the live Link for public consumption. If the board refuses to do anything, everyone in Machete will know what Cooper's done."

"Why would the public care if Cooper screwed Schramm over and stole his job? That's how the corporate world works."

Schramm said, "They'll care about the other part of what we found. That Cooper's been skimming money out of the company's public works fund to pay off the people he's been using to get me."

Reece pursed her lips and blew out a breath. "Yeah, they'll sure care about that."

The one thing corporations had to keep the people from rising up and overthrowing the unbalanced system was that each corporation had a public works fund that they donated to Akon's public services. How much they gave each year was published, and consumers paid attention. A bigger donation resulted in bigger sales, since people chose to buy products from companies that gave them more support.

Stealing from the public works fund would make Cooper Fields the most hated man on the planet. Further, Rexcare would suffer from public outrage that would likely result in boycotts.

A loud bang against the door made Reece jump and she turned to look at it.

"They're not getting through that," Schramm said. "It's reinforced to withstand a level-three bomb. If they get us, they'll come from there." He pointed upward.

Trey stepped further into the cavernous room. "What

is this?"

"Cooling room," Schramm said. "Big datacenters pull a lot of heat. I won't bore you with the details of siphoning the heat out while funneling in cool air and maintaining a balance between breathable air and a hardware-friendly environment."

"Are you sure?" Trey asked. "Because I got a little bored just when you were saying all that."

Marky snorted out a laugh, but Trey remained completely deadpan.

Schramm smiled. "You were the one who asked."

Trey shrugged and fitted the data stick into the reader. "So, we're doing this? It means blackmailing Rexcare's board. Can't say I love that."

Schramm nodded. "We're doing it. I don't love it either. I'd wanted to simply give them the proof and let it speak for itself. But sometimes, in the corporate world, blackmail is necessary."

"Okay," Trey said. "Just making sure. Here we go. One message to the board of directors, marked highest urgency."

Trey stared at the reader.

<Raya,> Reece sent via the group channel. <Where are you?>

<I ducked into the ladies' room for a few minutes. There was a lot going on in the halls. What happened?>

<We're holed up,> Reece replied. <Trapped, but secure. We're sending a big bomb to the board and we're hoping they respond without making us detonate it.>

<What can I do?> Raya asked.

<Go back down to the lobby. Ask to see Berg Raines. He

won't be in. Tell them you have an urgent message. Tell them you've sent it via the Link and will wait.>

<Wow. Okay. But everyone's okay?>

Reece looked to Trey, pretty sure he was the one Raya was asking about. *<Yes. All uninjured and currently safe. How's that looking for us, Apolla? How long would you say we have before they bust down on us?>*

Apolla answered, *<That's hard to judge. I see some heavy machinery moving to the floor above you, but that's about all I know. There aren't any security feeds in the crawlspace.>*

Reece looked to Schramm. If anyone knew about the structural limits of the building, it would be him.

He shrugged. "Don't look at me. I'm an executive, not a structural engineer."

Marky looked up at the ceiling, as if it might provide a clue. "I guess we'll have to wait and see. Either the board will respond and call off the dogs, or we'll at least see them coming."

Trey looked up suddenly, his eyes focusing on them. "It's sent."

Schramm nodded. "All we can do is wait." He straightened his shoulders. "What should we do to pass the time? I don't suppose Marky brought her King Sweep set."

Marky laughed. "Sorry, I didn't know I'd need it while committing theft and fraud and whatever else we've done."

Schramm grinned. "And I thought you were a die-hard gambler."

"Well…" she reached into her bag and pulled out a small rectangular object. "I do have some old-style playing cards. Have you ever played something called 'poker'?"

* * * * *

They had just gotten the rhythm of a game Marky called Seven Card No Peek when the group channel lit up with a message from Apolla.

<Guys, I've got something. I think we can get you out of there.>

Reece forgot about revealing her next card. <How?>

Apolla's answer came immediately. <It won't be easy. There's an old access vent you can pull open and climb up to get to an air maintenance crawlway. Once you get to the crawlway, it will be dusty and cramped, but fine. Getting there through the vent will take some effort, though.>

<How did you find it?> Marky asked.

<I pulled up some old schematics of the initial architecture. Comparing it to what I can see that now exists, it looks like a newer venting system was put into place and this old vent was simply covered over.>

<Tell us how to find it,> Schramm said. He looked like he was more than ready to get out of there.

Half a minute later the cards lay forgotten on the floor and Trey, Reece, Schramm, and Marky stood staring at a panel that was about Reece's height, minus her legs, and about the width of upper body with her elbows extended.

<Did you find it?> Apolla asked.

<It was right where you said,> Schramm answered. <But it's bolted up. I don't know how we're going to get into it

without a prybar or a torch.>

Trey ran his fingers around the panel, skimming its edges. Then he braced his feet, rounded his back, and wrenched the panel right off the wall.

He threw it aside, then grinned. "I am a prybar. Now let's get the hell out of here before security remembers that this access panel exists—because if we can get out, this is a way they can also get in."

It was a sobering thought.

<*We've got it open,*> Schramm said on the group Link. <*We're going to give it a try.*>

<*Just follow it. Then it opens up into the crawlway. When you get there, let me know and I'll lead you through,*> Apolla advised.

<*Understood.*> Schramm nodded to Marky. "You go up first. I'll follow you. Then Trey can follow Reece up, in case her leg gives her problems."

Marky caught her lip in her teeth. "What if there's something in there?"

Schramm shrugged. "It'd be better than what's eventually going to find us in here." He patted her on the shoulder. "This building isn't that old, so don't worry. I'll be right behind you."

He helped her step up to the edge and then into the vent.

Marky's voice come out muffled. "It's dark. Hang on. I have a light."

Reece heard faint sounds of shifting movement.

"Okay. There are rungs, but there are only about half as many as there should be. This will be interesting. Here I go." Marky's feet disappeared as she moved upward.

Schramm went in behind her.

After a few seconds, Marky called down, "Ah, there's a ledge."

A moment later, she sounded further away. "Ledge didn't last. More rungs."

Trey gestured to the opening. "Your turn."

Reece hoped her leg would do its job. She took a breath, stepping in, and immediately regretted it. Marky and Schramm had stirred up a whirlwind of dust. Reece stopped, squinting her eyes shut and coughing violently.

<*I hope you have some kind of superior breathing system in that chest of yours,*> she sent to Trey. <*This is unpleasant, to say the least.*>

<*Nope,*> he answered. <*Just regular old lungs.*>

To protect her eyes, she closed them to tiny slits, then used her visual display to enlarge that sliver of vision on a side panel. Then she looked at it rather than reality.

That helped her eyes, but there was no helping her lungs. She coughed the whole way to the ledge, then to the second set of rungs. She heard Trey behind her, climbing and coughing some, but not as much as her.

He probably did have some sort of advanced lungs, and he just hadn't wanted to admit it.

Reece's leg hadn't bothered her much from regular walking and running, but it took the opportunity to let her know that she had been recently shot. An aching burn spread up through her thigh, connecting the entry and exit points via the channel between. She gritted her teeth and ignored the pain.

"Keep moving," Trey ordered from below.

"I am," she insisted.

"Is it your leg?"

"No."

"It's your leg, isn't it?"

As she struggled to bring it up to the next rung, she sighed. "Maybe."

How many rungs could there be in here? Surely they had to arrive somewhere soon. But with only the use of her Link to brighten her way and Marky and Schramm ahead of her, she couldn't tell how much further that would be.

As she was struggling up the next rung, a firm pressure applied itself to her backside, taking her weight off her legs and pushing her upward. It was as if some levitating fairy had put her shoulder against Reece's butt to give her a lift.

Of course, there was no fairy, unless Trey counted as one, which she didn't think he did. Which meant he was getting a handful of a whole lot of her ass, but given the current situation, she wasn't going to complain.

In any case, she was certain he wasn't enjoying it, and that was good enough for her.

She heard Marky say something up ahead, and while Reece didn't understand the words, she heard the relief.

Four more rungs and they'd leveled out.

<*Apolla, we've arrived at the crawlway,*> Schramm reported.

<*Good. I was starting to get worried. Follow it as far as you can, then when it branches off, let me know. I'm trying to compare the original building's design with what's currently on file, which is outdated anyway. We might need a little trial and error to figure it out. But you're headed west at the*

moment, taking you away from that cooling room, and that's good. We need to get you out at some point that lets you get out of the building or establish a more defensible position.>

Schramm and Reece were the first to look up after listening to that long missive from Apolla. Marky's eyes came up next, and Trey looked up last.

She'd have to tease him later about being a slow reader.

"Same order?" Marky asked.

"I'll go first here," Trey said. "There might be junk that needs to be cleared, or it's possible we'll encounter people coming in this way. Better I'm out front for that."

They reversed order, with Trey leading, Reece following, Marky on her heels, and Schramm bringing up the rear.

Crawling through the narrow space wasn't awesome for Reece's leg, but she could manage it. There wasn't as much dust here, either, which was good.

Trey sent them all a group message. *<I'm at a junction. I can go north or south.>*

<Depends. Do you want your best shot at leaving the building, or at getting to a place they can't reach?>

Apolla's message caused them to look at one another.

Marky spoke first. "I vote for getting out. We can always come back after we know which way the board is going to decide."

Schramm shook his head. "I'm not leaving until I make them acknowledge that I'm not a criminal, or a traitor to my company."

"If he's out of Rexcare," Reece said, "then so am I, apparently. So I'm staying."

They all looked at Trey.

He shrugged. "My partner's staying, so I'm staying."

Reece looked sympathetically to Marky. "You helped us tremendously. You can follow the way out if you want to."

After a moment's deliberation, Marky shook her head. "I'm better off with all of you than without. I can't tear metal off the walls like some people."

<We're staying,> Schramm told Apolla.

<Go south, then. I'm going to send you some coordinates to a secure room. If you can get there, you can hold it indefinitely. Cameras show there's no one there, but it has double-reinforced walls and an internal locking mechanism.>

<The corporate retreat,> Schramm said. <At least that's what we call it. It's a bomb shelter, on the bottom level of the building, meant to protect against terrorist or retaliatory acts. If we can get in, I should be able to close and lock it.>

<They wouldn't have changed the codes and all that?> Reece asked.

<Since it's in my best interest to run and stay hidden, probably not. They wouldn't have thought they'd need to protect the shelter from me.>

Reece contacted Raya. <Raya, are you still out there? We're on the move to the safe room. You should either meet us there, or better yet, get yourself out of here and pretend you had nothing to do with it.>

Raya didn't respond immediately. Or within two minutes. As time ticked onward, Reece started to get worried.

Finally, a full six minutes after Reece's message, Raya responded. <Sorry. I was giving a talk on brand awareness to

a group of new exec recruits. I couldn't break my train of thought at the moment.>

<A what?> Reece asked. <Why?>

<Because someone recognized me and assumed that was why I was here. So I agreed that it was. I'm not coming with you. Go in without me.>

Reece was glad she had the good sense to preserve her reputation, in case all this went wrong.

But then Raya send another message. <I'll run interference for you, and once you're locked in, I can act as your proxy.>

Trey said, <No, you should get out. There's no reason for you to go down with us if all this goes wrong.>

<Don't worry. I'll tell them you contacted me because I happened to be in the building at the time. Just a happenstance that was convenient since you know me. I'll present myself as a neutral third party, as a fixer does. It will just be a professional showing off her skills and putting a rival corporation in her debt. Easy.>

Reece smiled. It was smart thinking.

<I still don't like it.> Trey conveyed a disapproving tone even as he crawled south ahead of her.

<When all this is done, you can give me a stern talking-to,> Raya answered. <Until then, move faster.>

He didn't respond, but to Reece, it felt like he'd sped up a little.

Apolla said, <You should be able to see junction numbers every time you pass one. Let me know what you're seeing so I can track your progress.>

They made it past 2E. Then 3F Then, later, 8G. Apparently, G had a lot of sections. They crawled until

Reece's knees went numb, and then came roaring back to life with a feeling like someone had been drumming on them with hammers.

At 7H, Apolla halted them.

<Good. There should be an access panel ahead of you. Open it.>

This one, at least, didn't have to be torn open. Trey was able to simply unlatch it.

<It's an elevator shaft,> he said.

<You can climb down it one level, where you can get out and take the elevator the rest of the way down.>

<Uh,> Marky said, <I don't feel good about climbing down an elevator shaft. If someone uses it, we'll be squashed.>

<I'll let you know if someone is boarding. Right now, it's sitting at the top, next to an executive suite. I'm guessing it's being kept there on purpose until the exec wants it.>

<And if he or she wants it while we're in there?> Marky asked.

<Don't still be in there,> Apolla advised. <Go fast. It's just one level.>

"Don't be in there," Marky muttered aloud, where Apolla couldn't hear her. "Of course! What was I thinking, when such a foolproof plan was available?"

Rather than argue, Trey simply stepped out and began climbing down. Reece followed. After a moment, Schramm appeared above her. She hoped Marky did, too.

About halfway down, the rungs vibrated slightly under her hands, making her breath catch.

<Is the elevator moving?> she demanded of Apolla.

<No. Why?>

<The rungs are shaking.>

<Something must have kicked on,> Apolla said. *<You're fine. Just hurry.>*

Trey helped her step out of the shaft, then did the same for Schramm and Marky. They replaced the panel and hit the elevator button. Reece held her breath that no other elevators arrived at this particular time.

<I can see you now,> Apolla reported. *<The elevator coming your way is unoccupied. There's no one down in the shelter, either. Your path is clear.>*

Reece felt like it was too good to be true. She continued feeling that way as they got in, rode down, and then exited on the shelter level.

As the elevator settled, she got a good grip on Righty and Lefty. Then she changed her mind and palmed her pulse pistol.

The doors slowly opened and Reece shoved forward, ready for a good offense to be their best defense.

But no one was there.

"Are we doing this wrong?" she demanded. "Is there some reason locking ourselves in the shelter is impossibly stupid? Why has no one thought we'd do this?"

Schramm put a hand on her shoulder. "Because we're smarter. And that's why we're going to win."

Marky grinned. A big, brilliant grin that she turned full-force on Schramm. "Oh, that clinches it. I like you."

Schramm blinked at her three times rapidly. "Ah. Okay. So...let's go." He pointed ahead, then without waiting, began walking.

He keyed in a code and offered his eye for a retinal

scan and the door clicked.

Trey opened it and they walked through.

"One more," Schramm said, locking the door behind him. "I'll just scramble this one and send the system into impending lockdown mode. But if no one's in the elevator right now, they can't stop us. They won't have time."

He got them through another door, and then they walked into the shelter.

"Are you kidding me?" Reece said, looking around as Schramm locked the door behind them and verified the final lockdown sequence.

She turned in place, staring. "This isn't a shelter. This is a luxury apartment. She stood in what looked like a large living room complete with sofas, chairs, a table, an open kitchen, and a wet bar. All of the furniture appeared to be fixed to the floor, but it was fancy stuff. Expensive.

She waved to four doorways. "Those are bedrooms, aren't they?"

"And a dining room, and bathrooms," Schramm replied with a nod. "And through the kitchen, there's a large warehouse with food and supplies to serve thirty people for a year."

Reece wasn't one to gasp, but this felt like a gasp-worthy announcement, so she gasped. "Wow."

She flopped down on a couch in a way she'd never do at home. "All this expensive stuff, and here I am, about to work a non-executive ass-groove into it.

She looked up to see that Schramm, Trey, and Marky were staring at her. "What?"

Trey shook his head. "You're just...you've always been kind of..."

"One of a kind," Marky said. She looked to Schramm. "So that's it? We're locked down? No one's getting in?"

"Nobody. Nothing unlocks this sucker short of the entire Orion Guard coming and blasting it open, unless we open it from the inside."

Reece rubbed her aching knees and let out a sigh. "Do those supplies have something to treat bruises? And how about some whiskey?"

Schramm smiled. "Yes, to the first. I'll have to take a look for the second."

"I'll come with you," Trey said. "I want to take a good look around."

Marky waved them off. "I'll check it out later. For now, I'll sit with Reece."

They watched the men go through a doorway and Reece sighed and dropped her head to the couch behind her.

"You're in worse shape than you're letting on, right?" Marky asked.

"I'll be fine. Especially now that we're done crawling. Do you mind updating Raya and Apolla? I'm going to have a little rest."

"Sure," Marky agreed. Then she sat up straight. "Oh, damn!"

Reece lifted her head, alarmed. "What?"

"I left my cards in that cooling room. We'll have to think of something else to do for the next year."

Marky was being funny, of course, but the idea of them actually being stuck down here for an extended period didn't sound too bad, after the past couple of months.

Then she remembered how much she didn't like living in close quarters with people, and how she tended to be kind of cranky, and most of all, that Kippy was on the outside.

She hoped the board responded to them quickly.

FURTHER ARRANGEMENTS
DATE: 06.06.8948 (Adjusted Gregorian)
LOCATION: Rexcare HQ, Ohiyo, Akonwara
REGION: Machete System, PED 4B, Orion Freedom Alliance

Reece and Trey spent a strange two days with Schramm and Marky in the shelter, waiting to hear from the board. Raya and Apolla had gone on standby, but checked up on them every so often.

Kippy was safe, but laying low. It was him that Reece worried about the most, at the time things had seemed like a slam dunk, but this waiting game was sure to be wearing on him.

Otherwise, they lived in a strange limbo of gourmet food, plush furniture, and existing in a self-imposed prison while the board determined their way forward.

"Two days is nothing to worry about," Schramm told them. "They know we're here, and not going anywhere, What's more, we can't make any trouble for them in here. We have no way to access critical systems. So we're simply in stasis, and they can get back to us once they've decided what's best for the company. They're probably also working on how they'll spin this whole thing, public relations-wise."

"It's a strange world you live in." Marky had her feet kicked up on a side table while Schramm made lunch in the kitchen.

Reece so enjoyed the sight of an exec working in the kitchen that she'd claimed the to need to rest her knees, which were already much better, to avoid helping.

"Not really," Schramm said. "It has its own rules and limits, like any other. But it comes with a lot of privileges that others do not."

"So it's worth it, then?" Marky put her feet on the floor and sat up to look at him.

"To me, it has been, given the alternatives. I like the work and I like the lifestyle. I don't love having so little time for personal interests, but that's the price that comes with the rest of it." Schramm dropped some onion into a skillet.

"You could have your own business, like me," Marky said. "Decide your own hours, do something that you like."

"Do you like everything about your job?" Schramm challenged. "Keeping customers happy, taking a loss sometimes, always knowing that if something were to happen, you could lose it all?"

"Well…no," Marky admitted. "But those are my tradeoffs for making the decisions."

"It's the same thing, with a different job title." Schramm shrugged.

"I guess." Marky fiddled with her spiky hair.

By the time Trey came out, drying his hair with a towel, Reece was helping put plates on the table. "That smells great."

"Leave it to you to show up when the work's done and the food's ready," Reece said.

"Lucky timing." Trey smiled innocently.

A little too innocently.

They had just started eating when Schramm's head popped up, his eyes unfocused.

Reece froze in place, her water glass in her hand.

After a moment, Schramm's head lifted and his eyes focused. "The board has agreed to hear our argument."

"What does that mean?" Marky asked.

"It means they're going to approach this matter as a trial. We'll present our side, Cooper Fields will present his side, and then they'll decide who to side with."

"But we have to come out of here to do that, right?" Trey asked. "It could just be a trick to get us out of here where they can grab us."

Schramm shook his head. "All contracts will be signed and registered beforehand. But we'll have to agree to be bound by the arbitration. That will be in there, too."

"I'm not excited about that idea." Marky looked deeply concerned.

"I'll assume your liability," Schramm said. "Whatever, if anything, they settle on you, will come to me instead. You can leave here safe and secure. I'll do the same for Apolla and Raya. Only Reece, Trey, and I will be at any risk."

Marky didn't look cheered by that. "I don't want you three to be at risk."

Schramm nodded. "I know, but this is how it's done. This is a good sign, really. We just have to do our part and show why they should find in our favor. We'll be back at work in no time."

It wasn't quite that simple, or such a foregone conclusion, but Reece didn't correct him. She wanted Marky to feel okay about going home. She was only there to help them, anyway. Reece felt it was right to assume the responsibility for her and the others.

"So what," Marky said, "we sign the arbitration papers and just walk out of here like nothing happened? Like I didn't hack into their system and suck a few kilos of dust into my lungs crawling through Rexcare's nooks and crannies?"

Reece nodded. "Yep. The rest of us will leave here, too, and go back to our lives. Well, other than not working, of course. We'll have some unpaid time off, but the arbitration date should be pretty quick. They don't like this kind of thing to affect the company, so they make an effort to get it behind them."

Marky pursed her lips. "It seems like such an unmemorable resolution. I kind of expected all this to wrap up with a big firefight and possibly an explosion or two."

Trey chuckled. "That was our last job."

Reece shook her head and winked at him. "It happens that way sometimes. But most of the time, it ends like this. Corporate, efficient, and entirely binding."

"Dull," Marky added. "Downright boring."

Considering recent events, a little bit of boring didn't sound so bad to Reece. "We'll see. Maybe we'll give them a little extra something to liven things up."

When Schramm and Trey looked at her reprovingly, she quickly added, "I mean of course we *won't*. But if we wanted to, we totally could."

They didn't seem entirely convinced, but Reece didn't care. She dug into her food with extra enthusiasm. If she got a chance to trouble the people who had given her trouble, she'd sure as hell do it.

She was good at making trouble, and could be patient, when she had to be.

* * * * *

Maybe she wasn't as patient as she thought. Reece had to wait an entire week for the Rexcare arbitration to begin, and in the meantime, she wasn't sure what to do with her time.

On day one, she gardened for Aunt Ruth, spent about fifty-eight hours scratching behind Rio's ears, and also gone to visit Dex at Trey hen Trey loud of a snort of la house just a short walk away. The poor monkey had been nearly apoplectic with excitement, hopping from Trey's shoulder to Reece's, as if unsure of how to best take advantage of this bounty of human companionship.

Trey showed her some of Dex's new tricks—shaking hands and playing dead. Reece wasn't sure it was appropriate to teach dog tricks to a monkey, but since Dex seemed thrilled with it, she decided it wasn't up to her to judge.

When Raya stopped by after work, Reece hung out with them for another twenty minutes, then made an excuse. No doubt Raya wanted Trey to herself.

As she walked back home, Reece thought of Kippy. She checked the time. It wouldn't be busy yet at the Ringtoad. She could go by and visit him. Would it be weird to be there, now that things had changed between them?

She'd just have to go see.

She sent her aunt a message so she wouldn't worry,

then walked right past her house and toward the Ringtoad. By the time she made it there, the back of her neck was slicked with sweat.

Kippy saw her as soon as she entered and grinned as if she'd just given him a present.

Yeah, that was kind of nice, she had to admit. He didn't smile like that for anyone else.

"Hey, Champ. You look damp."

She grinned. "You're must be in a good mood. It's been a while since I heard you rhyme."

"I'm glad you're here, and not full of bullet holes." He set a glass on the bar in front of her seat.

"It was just one bullet hole, but it's better."

He grabbed a bottle of H&P and poured her a generous portion. "And you get a five-day vacation until Rexcare clears you and you can get back to work, right?"

"That's a very optimistic summary, but yes, more or less."

"We could go to the beach," he suggested. "That was fun last time."

"It was. But I should stick around here, just in case something comes up."

He nodded, smiling. "Yeah. I knew you'd say no."

She tossed back half the whiskey. Ahhh. "How did you know? I could have said yes."

"Nope. Not with something hanging over you. You're too results-oriented for that."

She blotted her lips with a napkin. "Hm. True. So then why did you ask?"

"You look like you need a kick in the butt."

"I just got shot in the leg. Why would I need to get

kicked in the butt?" she demanded.

"You tell me."

"Because I don't like sitting around waiting for someone else to determine my future?"

He nodded, wearing a knowing expression.

She continued, "And I know there are things I can do to tip the balance?"

He nodded again. "Keep going."

"And the only reason I'm not doing anything is because most of the people I care about put themselves on the line for me, and I don't want that happening again."

"Because you don't want to be unfair to them," he said.

"Yeah." She finished off the whiskey.

"But consider this," he said, leaning over the bar. "Is it fair to risk your future, and therefore our ability to see you in the future, because you want to protect people who won't want to be protected?"

"Is it?" she asked.

"Is it?" he parroted.

"Or is it my job to take care of people I care about, even when they don't want it?" she asked.

"Hm," he said thoughtfully. "It's one of those."

She leaned forward until they were almost nose to nose. "You think I should."

"I do. You're the best at fixing, so why not fix your own situation?"

She smiled. "You just don't want me to end up unemployed and sitting here all the time drinking all your profits."

He tapped the end of her nose. "I'd gladly let you, if it meant you'd be here all the time. Though there would be all the liver disease to deal with."

She smiled. "I'd prefer to keep my liver in good shape."

"You'd better get to work, then."

She sobered and gave him a serious look. "Do you really think so?"

"You're Reece, corporate fixer. So go. Fix."

She nodded slowly. "Yeah."

She decided to stop feeling guilty for pulling her friends into her problems. If they had problems, she'd jump right in with them.

Kippy held up the bottle of H&P. "Another?"

She smoothed her hair. "Save it for next time. I need to get to work."

He grinned, his dimple sinking into his cheek. "Yeah, you do. And when you're done, you owe me that trip to the beach. A whole weekend this time, not just a day trip."

"You're on." She leaned forward over the bar to give him a long kiss and heard hoots and cheers from the staff and clientele.

Might as well let people know that this guy was hers, after all.

Feeling better than she had in quite some time, Reece stood, smoothed her weapons belt, and strode out.

She had work to do.

* * * * *

Should I call Trey?

The next morning, she was stuck with a conundrum.

She should call him. Of course, she should. He was her partner.

On the other hand, he had a few days ahead of him to relax, spend time with Dex and Raya. Considering what could happen if the board decided against them, it seemed uncool to take that time away from him.

What finally brought her to his doorstep was the fact that if he did something like this without telling her, she'd have been pissed.

They were partners. He at least deserved the chance to decide for himself how he wanted to spend the next few days.

Trey let her in, and while he made some tea, Reece played with Dex. First, he brought her everything small and shiny he could find. Then, they took turns making shooting gestures at each other with their hands, then pretending to die.

He was really good at it. The way he fell over backward with his hands on his chest looked better than the way people did it in the sims.

When she took her turn, he made a particular rolling chirrup that was high-pitched and went up and down in tone. People who didn't know Dex would probably think she was nuts, but she was certain it was his version of laughter.

"Here we go." Trey brought in a pitcher and glasses on a tray. He even brought a tiny cup for Dex and poured him some tea.

"He makes a mess, but if I don't give him his own tea,

he'll put his head in my cup," Trey explained. "And I've found I really dislike getting monkey hair caught in my teeth."

"Yeah…sounds like something I'd take a pass on, too." Reece grimaced.

"So what do you need to say?" he asked.

"Say?"

"You have something on your mind. I can tell."

"You've gotten to know me pretty well," she admitted.

"Yep. We've come a long way from you calling me offensive names and ditching me. But let's reminisce another time. What brings you here?"

"I have an idea. A way to make sure things go the way we want with the board."

His eyebrows rose. "What, a bribe? Blackmail? Taking someone out and hiding the body?"

"Kind of all of them, and yet none of them," she hedged. "It's a side of our work that I haven't yet let you see."

He shared a long, serious look with her. "Okay. Let's do it."

"Just like that? You don't want to know more about it?"

"If it's the job, and how things get done, and it ensures our future, yep. Let's go." He showed nothing but certainty.

"Okay," she said. "But I warned you. This is going to get ugly."

He nodded. "Don't forget, I've seen you first thing in the morning. Whatever it is, I can handle it."

* * * * *

Trey wore an expression of bafflement mixed with fascination, sprinkled with just a wee bit of horror.

"I thought we were going to kill someone," he said, his voice flat.

"Nothing quite that simple. This job rarely is," Reece said.

"I kind of feel like I should have told you no."

She nodded. "I suspected you'd feel that way. But there are times when we have to embrace the worst of the worst. And we're doing this for our future."

"Right. Our future."

He said the words like he was trying to convince himself, but was failing.

She couldn't blame him.

On the stage before them, an entertainment act unique to Akonwara played out.

Well, not so much entertainment as weird predilection, and it wasn't so much a stage as an old guy's broken down back porch.

Reece had known old Dale—as opposed to young Dale, or the now-imprisoned Stabby Dale—as far back as she could remember. He'd been a union leader in the days before the consumer public had realized that they had more collective power by voting with their money. Once that happened, the unions quickly disbanded because they'd been largely ineffective at changing anything anyway.

Dale remained a bit of a legend in Slagside, though.

People held him in high regard both for the fact that he'd worked tirelessly to make life better for the average Akon citizen, and also because he'd remained in Slagside even after he could afford to leave.

He always said that he belonged with the people who were like him.

Reece, on the other hand, had gotten out of Slagside as soon as she could, though she visited often.

Old Dale was always glad to see her and always very interested in the latest machinations of the corporations. He still had a keen mind, at the age of seventy-three, even though he tended to behave in ways that made it seem otherwise.

Such as now. Reece took a moment to take it all in.

Old Dale stood on his back porch, which had been in need of repair thirty years ago, and barely qualified as a porch anymore. The man never liked using his money for himself, though, preferring to dispense it among his community.

Trey could have handled the disrepair and the clutter. What he seemed entirely without words for was the sight of Old Dale standing shirtless and darn near pantsless, besides a pair of far-too-brief shorts, with his brown, very rounded belly greased up like a ball bearing.

He stood in an old washtub—the *old* old kind, from the days before water reclamation units. On his face was an expression of delight.

"Are we ready?" Old Dale asked.

"Oh, yes. Start whenever you're ready," Reece said.

Trey peeled his eyes from Old Dale long enough to

shoot a *what's happening* look at Reece.

Old Dale cleared his throat. "This one's an oldie, but a goodie. You'll know it right off, Reece my girl, but your big shiny friend there will probably be hearing it for the first time."

The old fellow raised his hands, seemed to be listening for something, then began drumming a rhythm on his greased belly.

Reece had thought Trey couldn't look any more bewildered, but she'd been wrong. He grew steadily more perplexed while Old Dale drummed with his hands, adding counterpoints with his feet in the washtub.

And then the singing began.

I used to be a young man
In a different time than now
Times were so much simpler
When I had that cow
I wish I could have kept her
From falling in that ditch
But gosh she sure did make one
Delicious sandwich

At that point, Old Dale got serious about the drumming. He bobbed up and down from standing to squatting, because the sound of the deep washtub changed the resonance of his belly-slapping.

Trey looked utterly astounded at this point, and mildly dismayed by the sight of Old Dale, his shiny belly, and the surprisingly agile squatting.

Trey sent her a message. Sort of.

<*I...what.........what?*> Was apparently all he could muster.

<*Hang on, I think he's gearing up for a big finish.*> Reece kept her eyes glued to Old Dale.

Sure enough, Old Dale did a bit of yodeling, raising his voice up to a howl, and on the final note, he hopped out of the washtub. Putting his left hand in his right armpit, he flapped his right arm to emit two distinctive sounds that were quite different than the belly-drumming from before.

Trey took a step backward and it was all Reece would do not to burst out in a laugh that was sure to conjure up tears of hilarity.

Instead, she clapped and hooted. "Well done, Old Dale! That's one of my favorites."

"Don't I know it, my girl. I chose it special for you. And I thought your friend might like it. He looks like he enjoys a good sandwich."

Reece gripped Trey's arm to bring him to reality. As amusing as his reaction was, they were here for a purpose.

<*I told you this job would get ugly,*> she reminded him. <*Pull yourself together.*>

Out loud, she said, "His name's Trey. He's my new work partner, and a very good friend."

Trey cleared his throat and nodded. "Glad to meet you, sir."

"Don't 'sir' me, my boy. I'm no exec. Why don't you two come in so we can cool off? Don't worry—I'll put on a shirt. This is just my performance outfit."

"Uhm…" Trey looked to Reece.

"Of course," she said. "It's hot as hell out here."

Old Dale's house was in better repair on the inside. Locals, including Reece, quietly did work on it for him when he wasn't looking. It was almost a community project, looking after Old Dale as well as he looked after them.

Trey looked relieved at the rustic but tidy interior of the house. No doubt he'd imagined something like the porch.

"Why don't you make some limeade, my girl, while I clean off the grease and get dressed. Can't properly have guests without my pants on, can I?" He shuffled away, moving more like a man of his age would be expected to, in comparison to his squatting efforts moments before.

"Obviously, he's never met your friend CooCoo," Trey said when the old man was out of earshot.

Reece laughed. "That's right, he wasn't wearing pants when you met him." She smiled fondly. "Good times."

"I wouldn't have called it that at the time," he said as she handed him a pitcher. "But looking back on it, it's a great story."

"You just described my whole life." She opened Old Dale's chiller and pulled out a sugar bin and candied lime rind, right where he always kept them.

"I'm not sure whether to feel sorry for you, or envy you." Trey filled the pitcher with water.

"Neither. It is what it is. That's just the approach of a Slagsider. Do the best with what you have."

"So this is where you're really from?" he asked in a quiet voice.

She'd seen him quietly studying the small, run-down houses and the untidy streets. He'd seen the people who lived outside—the roamers, as people called them, because it sounded much nicer than homeless.

"It is. This is where I learned how to live. I learned hard truths that taught me about hard work, pragmatism, and knowing when to cheat, as well as when to look out for others."

"You learned right." Old Dale reappeared, now dressed in a shirt and a much more proper pair of shorts. "You're the poster child for growing up in Slagside."

She smiled fondly. "I don't know about that. You're far better loved than I'll ever be."

He snorted. "Who said anything about love? I mean success. Survival."

She handed Trey the salt so he could add a pinch to the pitcher as she sliced some fresh limes. Old Dale was a lot softer inside than he pretended to be, and that was the side that she really needed to appeal to, while making her request seem like a mercenary one.

"Speaking of survival," she began.

"Ah, there it is. I knew you weren't just bringing your new boyfriend here to meet me." Old Dale sat down in a rickety chair with a groan.

Trey and Reece started at each other in horror.

"He's my partner. My friend. There's nothing romantic between us," she explained.

"Ah, good. Glad to hear it, no offense, my boy." Old Dale nodded. "I'm still rooting for Kippy."

The heat burning on her cheeks surprised her. Why should she be embarrassed? Was it because the old man had known that she and Kippy belonged together before she had?

"Actually…" she stirred the limes into the water with the salt and the lime rind.

Old Dale clapped his hands together. "Hah, you finally got together, didn't you? About damn time."

"Yeah, I guess we did."

"You guess?" he asked.

Trey spoke up. "She doesn't want to jinx it by being too specific."

"Ahh. I gotcha. Well anyway, you were about to cleverly segue into why you're here before I interrupted you." Old Dale waggled his fingers at her. "Continue."

"Right." She tried to remember how she'd been about to segue into it. The old guy had thrown her off with his talk of Kippy. "Oh! Right. You were talking about survival. I've been working at Rexcare for a while now, and I've seen a lot about how corporations work."

Old Dale nodded and Trey stirred the limeade.

"There's an opportunity right now. Not just for me, though it would benefit me and Trey both. But for everyone who isn't an exec. You know how powerful the threat of a company boycott is, and how it has changed everything from products to public policy."

Old Dale nodded again.

She wasn't sure if his silence was a good thing or a bad thing at the moment, but she forged ahead. "There's an opportunity to frame Rexcare right now either as a good company looking out for the public, or a bad one that deserves a boycott. I have one piece of legitimate dirt and one piece of potential propaganda that could be very bad for them in the public eye. I also have a piece of news that would make them look very good. We can create a PR crossroads for them, and demand a price to push people in the direction that makes Rexcare look good."

"And you have a personal stake in this, do you not?" Old Dale asked shrewdly.

"We do. A very personal one. But we can work this so that it benefits not just us, but all the average people."

"How?" he asked.

"We tell the people that there's a cure for the sunsickness cancer and Rexcare hasn't brought it to the people yet because of greed."

"And is that true?" he pressed.

"Yes, on both counts, but it's misleading, because they're just about to bring the product to market, and it will be very affordable due to some—" she broke off and corrected herself, "due to a benefactor. The greed bit has already been dealt with."

"By you?" Old Dale squinted at her.

"I did some negotiating," she admitted. The story with Dr. Fitzmiller and the research, of course, was much more complicated, but those details didn't matter.

"I see." He rubbed his chin with his thumb, looking thoughtful. "What does the public stand to gain from your proposal?"

"They're already getting the sunsickness cure, regardless. So that doesn't really count. But if we can push Rexcare the way we want, we can make them look good and protect them from some embarrassing information about a misbehaving executive that the public needn't know. And if that happens, Trey, my boss, and I get to keep our jobs and push that misbehaving executive out. Further, that misbehaving guy won't be in a position to perpetrate harm on people, while my boss is a relatively moral guy."

"Everybody's relatively moral, depending on their understanding of morality and their own rationalizations," Old Dale mused.

"That's true," she agreed. "But whose perception do you trust more—mine, or Cooper Fields?"

His eyes narrowed at the mention of the name.

"You know him," she said.

"By reputation, mostly," Old Dale said. "Is that limeade ready?"

Reece looked at Trey. He shrugged and pushed the pitcher toward her.

Apparently, he didn't feel like he was expert enough on the subject of limeade.

"Looks good," she told him. "Care to pour?"

He shrugged and filled three glasses.

Old Dale took his and sipped, looking contemplative. "Mm. This is good."

He fell silent and Trey looked to Reece, but she only gave him a tiny shrug. Old Dale would answer when he answered. There could be no rushing him.

Finally, he said, "Sounds like you've reasoned this through, and it makes sense for you, and for the public in general. It would even work well for Rexcare, if they go with your plan. But what's in it for me?"

Again, Reece simply waited.

Old Dale chuckled. "Not falling for that, are you?

Okay. You're good at what you do, and you certainly know Rexcare better than I do these days. Are you certain this is the squeeze you want to put on them, and are you certain innocent people won't get hurt as a result? I won't stick my neck out for anything that isn't in the interest of the public good."

Trey answered quickly. "The only real risk is to us. Reece, Schramm, and me. Admittedly, the public doesn't have a ton to gain from this, but they would get us at Rexcare instead of Cooper Fields, and we'd owe them a favor."

Old Dale smiled. "Ahh, but a favor owed from a powerful entity *is* a great deal to gain. It would be worthwhile even without that, but now I have to agree. What do you need from me?"

"A show of solidarity and support to prove to Rexcare we can deliver what we're threatening."

"And are you sure you have to threaten them to get what you want?" Old Dale pressed.

"No. We might be able to win without this. But why wouldn't we put the odds in our favor as much as we possibly can?" Reece met Old Dale's gaze as he watched her.

He nodded slowly. "Fair enough. I'll put the word out. We should have a big enough voice by tomorrow. Will that give you enough time?"

"And then some," Trey said, relief in his voice. "We have five days."

"Oh. By then, I could have half of Ohiyo formed up into an unruly mob for you," Old Dale said.

Reece grinned. "No unruly mobs, please. Innocent

people tend to get mixed up in them and someone always gets hurt. All we want is a mere threat, with some proof to back it up."

"Well, it's certainly a more boring way to go, but it's also less effort. Okay, then."

Reece relaxed. Old Dale would keep his word. He never agreed to something he wasn't willing to go all-in for. She took a long gulp of her limeade and found that it was, indeed, the perfect mix of sweetness and tartness.

"Now that that's settled," she said, feeling a wickedness seize her. "Why don't you perform *The Way to the Old Ugly Pig* for Trey? I think he'd like it."

She lifted her glass and turned her head to give Trey a gleefully villainous grin that Old Dale couldn't see. Truth be told, she loved his songs, although the belly part could be a bit much to handle. His songs were the music of her youth, and for once, her threadbare childhood was going to be of help to her.

THE DEAL

DATE: 06.07.8948 (Adjusted Gregorian)
LOCATION: Slagside, Ohiyo, Akonwara
REGION: Machete System, PED 4B, Orion Freedom Alliance

"I like Old Dale," Trey said on the way back to their neighborhood. "I think my musical tastes lie elsewhere, though."

"I won't tell him you said that," she promised.

He grinned. "Do all of his songs center around livestock?"

"Not all. He's got one about a smelly sock, and one about a washerwoman wife that's quite a barnstormer. But a whole lot of them are about animals. I don't know why."

Trey shrugged, so she did too.

"Think we have everything we need to push Rexcare to do what we want?" he asked.

"I think we've done everything humanly possible, and all we can do now is wait."

"That was some pretty Class-A fixing, by the way. I find I much prefer the underhanded wheeling and dealing part of this job to the part where people are shooting at us."

"Huh." She regarded him thoughtfully. "I've always preferred the hands-on stuff."

"This does not surprise me about you."

She shrugged and leaned her head against the headrest of her taxi seat. "Wake me up when we get there."

The movement of the vehicle had started to lull her to sleep when Trey gave a loud snort of laughter.

"What?" She opened her eyes to look at him.

"That one about the cow sandwich."

She grinned. "I knew you'd eventually come to love Old Dale's songs."

"Love is a strong word."

"You love them," she insisted.

"If you say so."

"I'm going to tell him the cow sandwich one is your favorite. He'll insist on singing it at your wedding, if you ever have one," she told him closing her eyes.

"Now you're just being mean."

Eyes closed, she simply smiled in response.

* * * * *

Reece liked winning.

She intended to win against Rexcare. As Marky would say, the cards were in her favor. All she had to do was play her hand.

Nonetheless, there was the possibility for things to go wrong. If they did, they'd go very, very wrong. She'd lose her career and without it, on Akon, she, Aunt Ruth, and Rio would have a hard time surviving. Trey and Dex would have the same problem, as would Schramm.

The stakes were high, and before she showed up to play the game, she wanted to make the most of the next five days.

Just in case.

She pushed through the items in her closet,

undecided. Considering she spent most of her time working, she had few things to dress up in.

A form-fitting black dress she sometimes wore to Rexcare company events seemed like her best choice. But then…why dress up?

She was who she was. She liked her black pants and tank, and her jacket. She liked her boots. If the real her wasn't good enough, then it didn't matter anyway.

After a little extra time on her hair and applying a shiny lip balm, she decided she was as dressed up as she was going to get.

Guns or no guns?

Guns, of course. She wore her weapons belt per usual. Whether or not it was legal for her to do so, she wasn't sure. She was neither an active Rexcare employee nor a suspended one. Technically. But she wasn't going to be parted from her Rikulfs without a major traumatic event.

Right. She was ready. She slung an overnight bag over her shoulder.

Rio sat on her nightstand, watching her with big, wide eyes. She rubbed his head and scratched his ears. "Good boy."

Downstairs, on her way out for the evening, she paused before she got to the door. Aunt Ruth looked up.

"Going out, dear?"

"Yes. I'll probably be out all night, so don't wait up."

"Okay. Have fun." Aunt Ruth smiled. Was there an extra glint of knowing in her eyes?

Reece had her suspicions.

She hurried out into the hot starslight of the waning perihelion day. Before too long, they'd move into the three-month night. Of course the planet's two artificial suns would give them a regular day-night cycle. Reece looked forward to having sunrises and sunsets again. There was something comforting about their daily cycles.

At the door of the Ringtoad, she hesitated. Was this too much, too fast?

Maybe, but that was how she did things. All in or all out. No in-between.

When she entered, she didn't see Kippy. Her heart dropped. Maybe he was in the back?

She hoped he was in the back.

She hesitated, then sat in her regular chair. Drumming her fingers on the bar, she waited impatiently.

He didn't show up.

"Hey, Reece," Skye, one of Kippy's regular bartenders greeted her. "Can I get you something?"

She could just order a whiskey. She could pretend that was all she was here for. She could wait and see if he showed up, or just go back home.

She could do a lot of things, but she wasn't going to.

"Hey, Skye. Is Kippy around?"

"He went to the cellar to do inventory. Did he know you were coming?"

"No, I just dropped in."

Skye nodded. "He might not be up for a while, so why don't you go down, if you don't want to wait?"

"Thanks. I will."

The stairway to the cellar was a little dark. She should remind Kippy to add some lighting. The temperature dropped quickly as she went down the stairs.

"We don't have as much rum as I thought we—" Kippy came into view and broke off when he saw her. "Hey. I thought you were Skye. Everything okay? I thought you'd be out working your nefarious magic."

She smiled. "All done. I've done everything I can. Now I just have to hope Rexcare sees things my way."

"That was quick." He stepped closer.

"That's how I operate."

"Really." It was just a word, but he somehow made it sound terribly suggestive.

What was the old saying? No guts, no glory?

She stepped closer and put her arms around his neck. "Really."

His teasing grin faltered, and he looked uncertain.

She leaned in and kissed him.

"You're not just here for a drink, are you? If you were, you'd already have it in hand." He skimmed his thumb over her cheekbone.

"You're right."

"Are you sure?"

"Well, you wouldn't have to twist my arm too hard to get me to have a drink." She tickled the back of his neck.

"No, I meant…"

She grinned. "I know what you meant. And yes, I'm sure."

He pretended to edge away. "Well, I don't know. This is all so sudden."

She laughed and the little bit of awkwardness she had melted away. "Yeah, just twenty-something years."

He nodded, putting on a show of being thoughtful.

"Well, when you put it that way, you do seem pretty convincing. I see why you're so good at your job. Let's go."

"Right now? You don't need to finish inventory."

"Oh. You're right. Here." He pulled her closer and gave her a long, slow kiss. "There. *Now* let's go."

Laughing, they ran up the stairs and out of the Ringtoad without saying a word to anyone.

* * * * *

"What is your defense?"

Reece had never sat in on an arbitration with the board. There had been times when she'd stood in front of the board to deliver a report, but only on two occasions. Mostly, the board of a corporation was almost a myth that lived behind closed doors.

Not today.

Reece stood straight, her chin high. "I don't need one. I acted in the best interest of my employer at all times, even when I was acted against by one of the company's own agents. In that light, I've been an exemplary employee who deserves to be rewarded, not punished. The same goes for my partner, Trey. We have both behaved to the highest standard in the company's best interest."

Molgen, one of the middling board members who tended to go along with the pack, said, "You call blackmailing us with the threat of exposure the highest standard?"

She met his gaze. "I do, when it is done in the

company's best interests."

"And organizing a potential boycott, and threatening us with that as well?" another middling board member asked.

"Yes." She looked at all twelve of them, one by one, taking her time. She locked eyes with each for a full two seconds before moving on to the next. "You hired me to be your fixer. I've done that. I've saved you, and given you the tools to become even more successful. The only question during this arbitration is whether you're worthy of the effort I've made on your behalf."

The room went silent. Had she gone too big with that statement?

Nah. She was fighting for her life here. Trey's and Schramm's, too. Even Erving's, in a way.

"To your knowledge," Janice began, "has Schramm Matthews ever acted in any way contrary to the company's interests? Keep in mind that nothing has been alleged against you, and there's nothing for you to gain by being loyal to him, if he is guilty of something."

Nothing was alleged against her? Apparently, they'd never realized she'd broken into their system to steal information about Rexcare's contract with Nizhoni at Hatchet & Pipe. And they also didn't seem to take issue with her breaking in to help Marky steal information to present to them.

Was Janice lying, or had they dismissed all of that as irrelevant?

Reece focused on Janice, the head of the board and therefore the most important person to convince. "Never. Schramm is the one exec I want to continue working with, because I can trust his devotion to Rexcare."

Janice exchanged a veiled look with Tillson and Jono, the other two top executives.

Down the hall, Trey and Schramm had been sequestered into their own rooms, to prevent them all from talking to one another about what happened in the boardroom. Had they been questioned already? Were her honest answers aligning with theirs?

"Very well. You may return to your waiting room. Please wait there without communicating with anyone inside or outside of this building, unless it happens in here. You are being closely monitored. If there's any food or other refreshment you'd like, you can let my assistant know on your way out."

Reece didn't leave the podium. "I'd like to say one more thing, since my livelihood depends on all this."

Janice paused, then nodded. "Go ahead."

"You all probably know I came from Slagside. It couldn't be more different than this place. This is where I chose to be, where to spend my life. It's where I can do what I do best, which is working as a fixer. But the one thing it doesn't have is a sense of unity. If anyone is to blame for what's happened with Cooper Fields and the trouble he's wreaked, it's whoever hired him, and whoever failed to know what he was up to. That means the responsibility belongs inside this room, not to anyone outside it." She ducked her head slightly.

"Besides me," she added. "Imagine I said that after I left. Okay, I'll go now."

On the way out, she told Janice's assistant, "I want a

steak as big as your head, cheesecake, sautéed mushrooms and onions, and some berry container-ice."

Then she stalked back to her sequestered room.

She'd done her best. Now she could only wait for the verdict.

* * * * *

The door to Reece's sequester room opened, yanking her into full wakefulness. After a massive lunch, she'd felt tired, and boredom had led her to stretch out on the comfy couch.

"What is it with you and sleeping?"

Trey's voice reached her and she bolt upright.

"What happened?" she demanded. She was standing. She didn't remember doing that.

A grin slowly spread across his face. "We won."

With a shout, she ran across the room and threw her arms around him. He picked her up and swung her around, both of them laughing.

"Swing me, too. It looks fun." Schramm stepped in behind Trey, looking amused.

"So we're all clear?"

"Way more than clear," Schramm said.

"What do you mean? Wait." She held up a hand and pointed at Trey. "Go ahead and swing him. I'll wait."

Schramm laughed. "I didn't actually—"

Too late. He was getting a thorough victory swing. The good news was that was he was laughing about it. He seemed a lot more like a regular person these days, like he'd loosened up.

Reece gave herself credit for that. "Okay, so what did they say?"

"Well," Trey said, "they talked a lot. Frankly, I tuned out for part of it. Blah blah, corporate buzzwords, you know. But the most important bit is that we're all clear and reinstated, and Cooper Fields is persona non grata from now on."

"Persona what?"

"He's done," Schramm said. "His life is effectively over, regardless of whatever happens to him next. No one will ever hire him."

"Good. So, what, do we just go back to work tomorrow?" She was ready for life to get back to normal.

"About that," Trey said. "Schramm turned out to be a pretty good negotiator."

She nudged Schramm. "Spill it. I'm dying here."

Schramm smiled. "You're looking at Rexcare's first sole CEO."

He put his arms out to his sides in a *check it out* gesture that made Reece grin because it was actually kind of sexy. She laughed, since she had never before seen him that way. All this appeared to have changed him.

"So then we're the fixers of the company's first CEO?" That sounded awfully good to her.

"Yeah, about that," Trey said.

She swatted his shoulder. "Stop saying that! Just tell me."

"It's kind of big. You might want to sit down."

Worry bubbled up in her. "We aren't regular employees?"

Trey shook his head. "No. I mean, we're fixers, sure. But we've become the thirteenth and fourteenth board members."

Okay, he was messing with her. "Hah. Good one. But seriously."

Trey laughed, and Schramm was chuckling too.

"It's true," Schramm said. "Well, mostly. The board wants you to be in charge of creating synergy between the company and Slagsiders. And they want you to keep your eyes on what's going on, so another person like Cooper Fields can't get anywhere in this company again."

"Creating synergy," she repeated. "It must be true, because it comes with corporate buzzwords. But...him," she pointed at Trey, then pointed at herself, "and me...execs? I'm dreaming. I got a bad steak and went into a coma. This isn't real."

Schramm said, "Well, you aren't a regular member of the board like the others. It's more of a liaison role, and you'll be treated more like junior executives than full members of the board. But you get the regular title, all the same. The rest will be written into your contracts. The legal team is working on that now."

She rubbed her forehead as they laughed at her. "But for all intents and purposes, I can say I'm an exec."

"Technically, yes," Schramm said.

"Okay, the mention of a legal team makes it sound more legit. So...it's real?"

"It's real," Trey said.

"Totally real," Schramm agreed.

"And there's a little bit more," Schramm said. "I had

time to think about life and what's good about living, and as CEO, my first official act is going to be that every exec gets three weeks of vacation every year. And now that you're execs, that includes you. *And*, the first week starts now. We all start back in our new positions one week from today."

She stared at him, still having a hard time believing it. She focused her attention on Trey. "How long was I asleep? And how are you acting so cool about this?"

He shrugged. "I'm just better than you, I guess. This is good, though. I'm going to have to look into what board members wear, and get some of that. And…you know…study up on what one does at board meetings."

Schramm patted his shoulder. "Don't worry about it. Board meetings are only twice a month and by special appointment. You don't have an officer role in the company, so it's not going to demand that much of you, most of the time. You'll still have plenty of time to handle your work as a fixer."

"Oh, that reminds me," Trey said. "I made a formal motion as a board member to hire Raya on. Not only would she be an asset here, but it's a good punch in the eye for Donnercorp to lose her. Win win."

"You made a formal motion?" Reece repeated. This was a lot to take in.

"Well…Schramm helped. But it's officially my motion."

Reece shook her head, smiling.

They stood looking at her, apparently waiting for something.

"What?" she asked. "I'm trying to get a handle on all

this."

"To be honest," Trey said, "I'm not really sure what to do now."

"Easy." Reece pointed at the door. "Go make a job offer to Raya."

"And what are you going to do?" he asked her.

"I'm…going to have Kippy meet me at my house and tell him and Aunt Ruth about it together. And I guess we should tell her that we're together, too." She couldn't help smiling, imagining it. She looked to Schramm. "What about you?"

He answered right away. "Some more time at the farmhouse. The tomatoes ought to be getting ripe."

She smiled. "Before you go there, what would you think about doing something else for a couple days? A celebration sort of thing?"

"What did you have in mind?"

She caught Trey's eye and he grinned. "I promised Kippy some sand between his toes."

"Beach trip!" Trey hooted.

"I'll invite Marky, too," Reece added slyly.

Schramm looked surprised. "Oh. Well, okay. It's been a long time since I've been to the beach. Why not?"

"That's the spirit!" Reece cheered. "This is going to be fun."

* * * * *

The benefit of rolling exec-style was being able to rent a stretch of private beach that they didn't have to share with anyone. Not having people tearing by and throwing sand on Reece's blanket was a luxury she could get used to.

She and Kippy lay stretched out under the shade canopy, enjoying a gentle breeze and complete, lazy, idleness. A few months ago, she'd probably have been bored, but she now realized the delight of having nothing crying for her attention.

Well, other than Dex. The little monkey hopped onto her stomach and nonchalantly clambered up to stand on her neck and show her something he'd found.

She spat out the grains of sand that he shook out of his fur and dropped onto her face. "Ugh. What did you find now?"

He liked seashells, but he liked shiny things even better. She twisted sideways so she could sit up. After she'd dusted herself off, she accepted what he held out to her with both paws.

"It's just a piece of plastic, Dex." She handed it back to him and he scooted away to add it to his pile of treasures.

Kippy sat up beside her. "Does he ever get tired?"

"Eventually. Then he pretty much just falls over wherever he is and sleeps the sleep of the dead."

A few meters ahead and off to the side, Schramm and Marky teamed up against Raya and Trey in what appeared to be a fiercely competitive game of sand bowling. She couldn't tell who was winning, but she was pretty sure she could have beaten the swim shorts off of all of them.

She was a champ at sand bowling.

Someday, when the timing was just right, she'd reveal

that fact and stomp all of them. Until then, she'd bide her time.

It was always good to hold back an ace for a time when she really needed a winning hand.

"You look happy," Kippy said.

"I'd be happier if I had a container-ice."

He grinned. "Not-at-all subtle hint taken." He twisted around and reached into the cooler, then faced her again, offering a packet.

Berry flavored, just like she liked.

She gave the package a twist and felt the coldness spread as it froze the liquid inside.

"I'm glad we have another day before we have to get back," Kippy said. "Though I'd be even happier if we got to spend a whole week out here."

"Another time. With three weeks of vacation and the inevitable lulls between jobs, I'll be able to carve out the time if you can."

"Oh, right," he said. "I have a business. Darn. Almost forgot about that."

She smiled and shook her head at him as she took a bite of container-ice. His business did very well, thanks to his hard work and dedication. His good looks and winning personality didn't hurt a bit, either.

"You know," she said thoughtfully, "I might have to start getting jealous when you flirt with someone at the bar now."

"Yeah? I'm okay with that. In fact, I might kind of like it."

"What if I start a fight?"

"Why is everything about fighting with you?" he

asked, exasperated but amused. "You cannot fight with any customers that didn't already want to fight. And I thought we'd talked about you branching out from all the fighting stuff, anyway."

"Right, you said I need to grow up."

"Not exactly," he said. "But close enough."

"I guess I should give up bar fights, except for in extreme cases when it's unavoidable, since I'm an exec now. I need to develop some of that stern robotic executive attitude."

"Please don't," Kippy said. "You're supposed to represent our kind of people, right? So be yourself, not one of them."

"Really?" She looked at him in surprise. "I thought you'd be totally supportive of the idea of me acting more respectable."

"I *like* that you aren't respectable." At her sound of mock-outrage, he quickly added, "I mean, I like that you're entirely yourself, and not emulating the people around you. It's why being a fixer suits you so well."

"So you like me just the way I am?" she asked.

"Well, mostly. It would be cool if you'd start liking a cheaper whiskey. I have to work extra hours just to support your H&P habit."

"Never! Let's just break up now," she announced, laughing.

"Oh! That's not even funny." He snatched the rest of the container-ice out of her hands, squeezed the remainder of it into his mouth, and stared at her combatively, his cheeks slightly puffed out.

He was too cute. She leaned forward, gave him a

smooch, then got up and ran toward the water, knowing he'd be immediately be on her heels.

After playing in the water for ten minutes, they scurried back to the canopy for relief from the sun. Even with their application of sun repellant, it was just too much to take for long.

The game of sand bowling between the other two couples had gotten to its final stages, and each roll of the ball elicited both cheers and groans.

"Here. Before they get back. I want to give you something," Kippy said, reaching into the bag he'd brought.

"Is it a new container-ice? Because you ate most of mine."

"No, but I'll get you another in a minute. Here." He turned back around, holding out a necklace.

It was the piece of sea glass Dex had brought her when they were at the beach the first time. Someone had polished it, making it glow like an emerald. The glass had been mounted into a gold backing and hung from a chain.

It was the best present anyone had ever given her.

She turned and lifted her hair so he could put it on her. Its weight settled nicely on her chest.

"I love it. Thank you." She leaned into him for a long hug that turned into more of a snuggle.

"I thought it would remind you, when you're working, of what's waiting for you when you're done with work. And maybe that will convince you to work less and play more."

"If you're not careful, you'll end up having to beg me

to leave your house and go work. I might turn into a terrible, lazy slob."

"I doubt it," he chuckled. "But I'd like to see you try."

A final cheer and groan went up, signaling the end of the sand bowling. Schramm and Marky had clearly come out the victors, in a surprising twist. Trey and Raya approached the blankets and chairs complaining bitterly about having been robbed.

"What was the bet?" Kippy asked.

"Who says there was a bet?" Trey returned.

Kippy and Reece simultaneously pointed at Marky, whose mere presence ensured that betting would be involved.

Trey exhaled an overly dramatic sigh. "Raya and I have to perform a song about a cow and a sandwich."

Kippy lit up. "One of Old Dale's songs?"

Trey sighed for real this time. "That's the one. No grease or belly-slapping. Just the song. But still."

An incoming message blinked at the left of Reece's vision. Based on Trey's expression, he'd gotten it, too.

She accessed it.

Janice at Rexcare had detailed some product testing of a cosmetic treatment that had shown some negative side effects. The board had been scheduled to convene the next day in an emergency meeting on how to handle the problem. They'd need to determine what to do with the product and how to handle the damage control. Things like this had a tendency to get leaked.

There would be people to pay off and threats to make.

Reece supposed that now that she was a board member, she'd be doubly bound to respond quickly.

With great power came great responsibility.

Technically, she didn't have great power, but she did have a great title, and it worked out to the same thing in the end.

She'd have to head back to Rexcare's headquarters today, rather than tomorrow. She felt disappointment, thinking of the fun she'd miss.

Kippy wore a knowing expression. Clearly, he already suspected what was happening.

"Sorry," she said to him. "We're going to have to get to work. A bit of an emergency."

He put his arm around her shoulders. "It's fine. We'll come back another day."

Schramm looked to Raya. "You should come, too. You haven't signed your employment contract yet, but since we all know it's a done deal, we can see if we can rush that along so you can help out with this one."

Raya nodded, standing to start shaking out the blankets and folding them. Trey and Kippy started folding up the chairs, while Reece and Schramm began dismantling the canopy.

In spite of the sudden change in plans, the mood of the group as they rode back remained good. How could it not be when things had turned out so well for all of them?

"You know," she said to Trey along the way, "it's been a while since we did a security checkup on Smooth. We should do that."

She'd have to come up with something new. Sequoia and Reggie had gotten good at countering her raids.

"You just want to punch someone in the dick," Trey

said. "You're not fooling me."

She laughed. Dick-punching had become a bit of a joke among her, Trey, Reggie, and Sequoia, due to the training session where the phrase had been coined.

"That's right," she agreed. "Dick punching is my favorite. Just like being a bandit assgrabber is yours."

Trey groaned as Raya peered at him quizzically.

Raya said, "Oh, I'm going to have to hear that story. And the dick-punching one, too."

"Thanks," Trey said to Reece sourly. "Thanks for that. See if I confide in you ever again."

Reece grinned because Trey knew he would. They'd be partners for a very long time, along with this band of motley, wonderful friends they'd collected along the way.

She looked forward to it.

Pineapple.

THE END

* * * * *

Reviews are the lifeblood of a book. Amazon promotes books that get reviews and it keeps them at the top of lists without authors having to spend money on ads and promotions.

If you liked this book, and are enjoying the adventures of Reece and Trey, please leave a review, it means a lot to us.

Also, if you want more Aeon 14, plus some exclusive perks, you can support me on Patreon (www.patreon.com/mdcooper), or join the Facebook Fan Group (facebook.com/groups/aeon14fans).

Thank you for taking the time to read *With Guns Blazing*, and we look forward to seeing you again in the next book!

THE BOOKS OF AEON 14

Keep up to date with what is releasing in Aeon 14 with the free Aeon 14 Reading Guide.

The Intrepid Saga (The Age of Terra)
- Book 1: Outsystem
- Book 2: A Path in the Darkness
- Book 3: Building Victoria

- The Intrepid Saga Omnibus – *Also contains Destiny Lost, book 1 of the Orion War series*

- Destiny Rising – *Special Author's Extended Edition comprised of both Outsystem and A Path in the Darkness with over 100 pages of new content.*

The Orion War
- Book 1: Destiny Lost
- Book 2: New Canaan
- Book 3: Orion Rising
- Book 4: The Scipio Alliance
- Book 5: Attack on Thebes
- Book 6: War on a Thousand Fronts
- Book 7: Fallen Empire (2018)
- Book 8: Airtha Ascendancy (2018)
- Book 9: The Orion Front (2018)
- Book 10: Starfire (2019)
- Book 11: Race Across Time (2019)
- Book 12: Return to Sol (2019)

Tales of the Orion War
- Book 1: Set the Galaxy on Fire

- Book 2: Ignite the Stars
- Book 3: Burn the Galaxy to Ash (2018)

Perilous Alliance (Age of the Orion War – w/Chris J. Pike)
- Book 1: Close Proximity
- Book 2: Strike Vector
- Book 3: Collision Course
- Book 4: Impact Imminent
- Book 5: Critical Inertia (2018)

Rika's Marauders (Age of the Orion War)
- Prequel: Rika Mechanized
- Book 1: Rika Outcast
- Book 2: Rika Redeemed
- Book 3: Rika Triumphant
- Book 4: Rika Commander
- Book 5: Rika Infiltrator (2018)
- Book 6: Rika Unleashed (2018)
- Book 7: Rika Conqueror (2019)

Perseus Gate (Age of the Orion War)
Season 1: Orion Space
- Episode 1: The Gate at the Grey Wolf Star
- Episode 2: The World at the Edge of Space
- Episode 3: The Dance on the Moons of Serenity
- Episode 4: The Last Bastion of Star City
- Episode 5: The Toll Road Between the Stars
- Episode 6: The Final Stroll on Perseus's Arm
- Eps 1-3 Omnibus: The Trail Through the Stars
- Eps 4-6 Omnibus: The Path Amongst the Clouds

Season 2: Inner Stars
- Episode 1: A Meeting of Bodies and Minds
- Episode 3: A Deception and a Promise Kept

MACHETE SYSTEM BOUNTY HUNTER – WITH GUNS BLAZING

- Episode 3: A Surreptitious Rescue of Friends and Foes (2018)
- Episode 4: A Trial and the Tribulations (2018)
- Episode 5: A Deal and a True Story Told (2018)
- Episode 6: A New Empire and An Old Ally (2018)

Season 3: AI Empire
- Episode 1: Restitution and Recompense (2019)
- Five more episodes following...

The Warlord (Before the Age of the Orion War)
- Book 1: The Woman Without a World
- Book 2: The Woman Who Seized an Empire
- Book 3: The Woman Who Lost Everything

The Sentience Wars: Origins (Age of the Sentience Wars – w/James S. Aaron)
- Book 1: Lyssa's Dream
- Book 2: Lyssa's Run
- Book 3: Lyssa's Flight
- Book 4: Lyssa's Call
- Book 5: Lyssa's Flame (June 2018)

Enfield Genesis (Age of the Sentience Wars – w/Lisa Richman)
- Book 1: Alpha Centauri
- Book 2: Proxima Centauri (2018)

Hand's Assassin (Age of the Orion War – w/T.G. Ayer)
- Book 1: Death Dealer
- Book 2: Death Mark (August 2018)

Machete System Bounty Hunter (Age of the Orion War – w/Zen DiPietro)
- Book 1: Hired Gun
- Book 2: Gunning for Trouble

- Book 3: With Guns Blazing (June 2018)

Vexa Legacy (Age of the FTL Wars – w/Andrew Gates)
- Book 1: Seas of the Red Star

Building New Canaan (Age of the Orion War – w/J.J. Green
- Book 1: Carthage (2018)

Fennington Station Murder Mysteries (Age of the Orion War)
- Book 1: Whole Latte Death (w/Chris J. Pike)
- Book 2: Cocoa Crush (w/Chris J. Pike)

The Empire (Age of the Orion War)
- The Empress and the Ambassador (2018)
- Consort of the Scorpion Empress (2018)
- By the Empress's Command (2018)

Tanis Richards: Origins (The Age of Terra)
- Prequel: Storming the Norse Wind (At the Helm Volume 3)
- Book 1: Shore Leave (in Galactic Genesis)
- Book 2: The Command (July 2018)
- Book 3: Infiltrator (July 2018)

The Sol Dissolution (The Age of Terra)
- Book 1: Venusian Uprising (2018)
- Book 2: Scattered Disk (2018)
- Book 3: Jovian Offensive (2019)
- Book 4: Fall of Terra (2019)

The Delta Team Chronicles (Expanded Orion War)
- A "Simple" Kidnapping (Pew! Pew! Volume 1)
- The Disknee World (Pew! Pew! Volume 2)
- It's Hard Being a Girl (Pew! Pew! Volume 4)
- A Fool's Gotta Feed (Pew! Pew! Volume 4)

MACHETE SYSTEM BOUNTY HUNTER – WITH GUNS BLAZING

- Rogue Planets and a Bored Kitty (Pew! Pew! Volume 5)

ALSO BY ZEN DIPIETRO

Dragonfire Station
- Book 1: Translucid
- Book 2: Fragments
- Book 3: Coalescence
- Intersections (Dragonfire Station Short Stories)

Omnibus Books 1-3 Edition: Lost Alliance

Mercenary Warfare
- Book 1: Selling Out
- Book 2: Blood Money
- Book 3: Hell to Pay
- Book 4: Calculated Risk
- Book 5: Going for Broke

Chains of Command
- Book 1: New Blood
- Book 2: Blood and Bone

ABOUT THE AUTHORS

Zen DiPietro is a lifelong bookworm, dreamer, and writer. Perhaps most importantly, a Browncoat Trekkie Whovian. Also red-haired, left-handed, and a vegetarian geek. Absolutely terrible at conforming. A recovering gamer, but we won't talk about that. Particular loves include badass heroines, British accents, and the smell of Band-Aids.

Subscribe to Zen's newsletter to be among the first to hear about sales and new releases.
(zendipietro.com/subscribe-to-my-newsletter)

* * * * *

Michael Cooper likes to think of himself as a jack-of-all-trades (and hopes to become master of a few). When not writing, he can be found writing software, working in his shop at his latest carpentry project, or likely reading a book.

He shares his home with a precocious young girl, his wonderful wife (who also writes), two cats, a never-ending list of things he would like to build, and ideas…

Find out what's coming next at www.aeon14.com

Made in the USA
San Bernardino, CA
03 November 2018